The Partnership

Written by Bruce Smith

Hidden Shelf Publishing House
P.O. Box 4168, McCall, ID 83638
www.hiddenshelfpublishinghouse.com

Cover Art: Diana Smith
Graphic Design: Kristen Carrico
Interior Layout: Kerstin Stokes
Editor: Robert D. Gaines

Publisher's Cataloging-in-Publication data

Names: Smith, Bruce L., author.
Title: Legend keepers : the partnership / Bruce Smith.
Series: Legend Keepers
Description: McCall, ID: Hidden Shelf Publishing House, 2022. |
Summary: For his sixth-grade science project, Garson climbs to the Shining Mountain Glacier in the wilderness not far from his home. His chance encounter with Buddy, a mountain goat, changes everything as their lives become entwined.
Identifiers: LCCN:2022909679 | 978-1-955893-08-4 (hardcover) | 978-1-955893-07-7 (paperback) | 978-1-955893-09-1 (Kindle) | 978-1-955893-10-7 (ebook)
Subjects: LCSH Mountain goats--Juvenile fiction. | Climactic changes--Juvenile fiction. | Glaciers--Juvenile fiction. | Friendship--Juvenile fiction. | Human-animal relationships--Juvenile fiction. | Montana--Juvenile fiction. | BISAC JUVENILE FICTION / Animals / General | JUVENILE FICTION / Science & Nature / Environment
Classification: LCC PZ7.1 .S65 Le 2022 | DDC [Fic]--dc23

Table of Contents

"There is always a moment in childhood when the door opens and lets the future in."

– Graham Greene, *The Power and Glory*

Chapter 1
The Big Day

Saturday, September 14

Garson wondered if the car might shake to pieces. From studying his map, the day before, he knew the road snaked up the mountainside. But a map can only tell you so much. Next to the legend's symbol for the road—a double-dashed line—were the words "unimproved dirt." It should have read "bone-jarring."

Strangling the Subaru's steering wheel, his mother's knuckles matched her face. Both were parchment white. It was one of those roads on which you either held your mouth open or clenched it shut. Nothing in between. Otherwise, when the car struck the next rock or rut, your teeth clacked together. Definitely unimproved!

"How much farther?" Garson's mother asked as the car splashed through a pothole disguised by overnight rain.

He scanned the map spread across his lap. "It's a ways."

She cast a searching glance his way. "What's a ways?"

"Um," he stared at the lines on the map. "There's still quite a few switchbacks to go. But then we'll be at the trailhead." His lips pursed with excitement.

The car clunked over another rock. She gripped the wheel tighter if that were possible. Despite zigzagging along at only ten or fifteen miles an hour, she couldn't avoid them all.

"I don't know," she said anxiously. "Maybe we should turn back."

It wasn't quite eight o'clock on Saturday morning. Mrs. Strangewalker had hoped Garson would change his mind about this outing. Navigating punishing roads to wilderness trails wasn't her thing. As the car lurched and lumbered up the US Forest Service road, she really wanted to be home. She'd be happy to toss a Frisbee in their yard or hike with Garson in the nearby woods. Anything but this.

But she also knew how much this sixth-grade science project meant to him. It had brightened Garson's life. Since school had started—something he used to dread—he had changed. He was happier this year. Now, when she asked at dinner about his day at school, he answered with details, not the usual "Okay." And those details were always about two things—his science class and his science teacher, Mr. Rock.

"No, Mom. I've gotta do this."

"Of course," she replied. "I just hope this old car holds together a little longer."

A grinding screech followed as the car pitched over a rock. "I'd better see if anything's wrong," she gasped while braking the car to a halt.

"I'll look." Before she could reply, Garson was out the door and disappeared beneath the Subaru.

After a minute or so, he plopped back in his seat. "Looks okay. Nothin leaking or hanging down."

"Did you check the muffler?"

"Yeah, the baling wire's still holding it up," he quipped while wiping mud from his sleeve.

I've gotta get that fixed, she thought. She smiled remembering Garson teasing her, "Instead of an Outback, your Subaru oughta be called an Outdated or a Worn Out."

Yes, she really needed a new car. But despite its age and odometer reading 155,000 miles and counting, she couldn't. She had to hold on to it a little longer.

Since becoming a single parent, life had become a struggle. Not that it wasn't before, never certain if Garson's father would return from his next deployment. Between her income as a part-time producer at the local TV station and her husband's pay, they were doing all right financially. Her struggle was about being a single parent. Second-guessing if she was doing things right, the way she and John would have done them together.

Each creak of the car was another reminder of how much she missed her husband. They had planned to replace the Subaru with a brand-new car of her choice. They intended to buy it after he returned from Afghanistan. But then...

When Marines wearing dress blue uniforms knocked at her door, she felt the air sucked from her chest.

"Mrs. Strangewalker?

"Yes," she said in a fearful whisper.

"I'm Captain Anderson. This is First Sergeant Jiggs and Chaplain Kennedy. May we come in?"

Unable to speak, she took a step backward to let them inside.

"Tell me. What is it?" she was trembling from her lips to her legs.

"Please have a seat," the captain gently took her elbow and guided her to a dining room chair.

As soon as all were seated, he began. "I've been asked to inform you that your husband has been reported missing in action during combat actions in Anbar Province, Afghanistan."

She shrieked, "No, not John!"

"We only have limited details," he continued. "Your husband was leading a patrol when enemy forces overwhelmed their position. Efforts to rescue survivors and recover the bodies of the fallen failed to find Captain Strangewalker. As of now, he's considered missing in action."

Everything inside her collapsed, like when the knot in a balloon comes untied. Untied. That was it. She felt untied from reality. This couldn't be happening. It just couldn't be true. She clutched her hands so tightly it hurt. She stared from one stranger to the next, seeking some glimmer of hope.

Garson came in the back door when he heard her scream. Glimpsing the men in uniform, dread shot through him. He remained beyond their view in the kitchen. As they talked in the dining room, he slouched to the floor, pulled his knees to his chest, and clasped his hands over his ears.

Captain Anderson told her what few additional details he had. "The Marine Corps is making every effort to find your husband. And of course, we'll keep in touch about his status." He slid a card across the table. "Please call with any questions, anything at all that we may help with in the meantime."

The captain paused, then added, "Captain Strangewalker was a highly trained and skilled officer. He knows how to take care of himself until we find him."

The chaplain led them in prayer, added some words of comfort, and suggested he could contact her clergy member who could provide support for her and her son.

The three men rose from the table and let themselves out the door. After they left, she realized she had failed to say goodbye. It was all too much to process.

When she looked up from the table, Garson was standing there, tears streaming down his cheeks. She leapt up and hugged her son until they'd both run out of tears.

Chapter 2
Lupine Lake

"Watch out!" Garson shouted, the Subaru lurching back to the center of the roadway. "Mom, are you okay?"

"Yes ... yes. I'm fine," she sucked in a breath, visibly rattled.

"You almost went off the side of the road. It's a long way down through those trees to the bottom."

"I'm sorry I scared you," she muttered, trying to erase thoughts of that day five years ago. *Five years, two months, seven days.* She never lost track.

Another half-hour and the road ended at the parking lot. It was more like a wide spot in the road with enough space for a few cars to park. No others were there. Fastened to a wooden post was a dark brown trailhead sign. Its faded yellow lettering read "Lupine Lake 1.5 miles."

Garson's heart began to race. *That's what Mr. Rock said I'd find.* The ear-to-ear smile on her son's face warmed her heart.

The sign mentioned nothing beyond the lake. But in his daypack, a Ziploc bag held a neatly folded second map. Mr. Rock had used and made notes on the map forty years ago. He gave it to Garson to do his science project. On it were all the details he would need.

"Just barely," she smiled, noticing the temperature gauge in the instrument panel was bumping the red danger zone. Color was returning to her knuckles.

It was shortly after 8:30. Enough time, Garson hoped, to make it to his destination and back. He knew it depended more on her than on him. Her idea of being outdoors was beach time, picnics, or a walk through the woods behind their home. But climbing to a mountaintop? That was a huge stretch.

When she learned what his science project required, she had braced herself for this day. No way would she let him hike there on his own.

She'd bought hiking boots and walked the neighborhood to break them in. She filled the daypack that she used to lug stuff back and forth to work with essentials for their hike: ball cap, scarf, lip gloss, gloves, etc. She felt prepared.

From his topographic map, Garson knew the climb was steep. He reminded his mom before they left their house that morning, "Do you have your puffer?"

It's what they both called the inhaler she relied on to control her asthma. Still, he wondered how she would do. Today would be no walk in the park.

After running through a mental checklist, Mrs. Strangewalker locked the car. She zipped the keys into the small outside pocket of her pack. The fabric's bright fuchsia color made her smile. Her ponytail of strawberry blonde hair spilled over the pack as she slipped her arms through the shoulder straps.

She beamed at Garson. *Maybe this will be fun.*

They both wore fleece pullovers, hers sky blue and his black. Mrs. Strangewalker wore stonewashed jeans loose enough for hiking. Garson wore a pair of faded-black cargo pants, his favorite color.

Beyond the sign lay a trail sprinkled with orange pine needles and hugged by conifer trees. "Do you want to lead?" Garson offered.

"No, you go ahead." She didn't want him to think she couldn't keep up, which was exactly what he believed.

They chatted about the smell of evergreen and the twittering of birds. "Chickadees and juncos," he said. Garson had acquired his dad's interest in birds. The well-worn field guide his dad gave him was stuffed in Garson's daypack. A baseball cap with an Audubon Society logo, that his mom had bought him, was snugged over his mop of coffee-colored hair. The hat's bill shaded his thin face and dark brown eyes.

"Except for those chirping birds," she said, "it's totally quiet. Sooo peaceful."

Conversation wasn't always easy. Since the day the Marines came to their house, a dark cloud had hung over them both. Somewhere deep inside Garson, a flame kindled hope. Somehow, some way, his dad would come back. Maybe his mom felt the same. He'd never asked, although he knew it's why she'd put off getting a new car, among other things.

He paused and turned to face her, "Mom, thanks for doing this with me."

His words made her day.

About halfway to Lupine Lake, the trail steepened. She stopped, "Look, Garson. Huckleberries. Here." She handed him several.

"Thanks."

Yeah, they're tasty. But that's not why she's stopping, he thought. As he turned and walked away, he heard, "Puff ... puff."

Her first hits on the inhaler. Garson pretended not to hear.

An hour after leaving the Subaru, they glimpsed Lupine Lake. Its shimmering blue water reflected a rising forest of green beyond. But the mountain's distant summit remained hidden somewhere above.

"This is so lovely, Garson. Like a postcard."

"Yeah," he agreed. It was amazing. But he really wasn't

thinking about the view. He was thinking about the climb that lay ahead. *Getting all the way up there and back is going to take a long time. Especially at the rate we're going.* He feared the rest was way more than his mom could manage.

"Let's enjoy this," she urged. "We could sit on that log and have a snack."

Reluctantly, Garson followed her to a driftwood log washed onto the shore. The smooth, gray trunk looked inviting. It made a perfect spot for a lakeside picnic.

Garson anxiously gazed across the lake to the mountain's tree-covered slope. His destination was somewhere up there. He fought the urge to tell her, *We don't have time for this. We can snack while we hike.* But he didn't say anything.

Mrs. Strangewalker rustled through her pack in search of granola bars. Out came a blue scarf, gloves, cell phone case, zip-locked sandwich, then a crumpled baseball cap she tugged onto her head.

Watching, Garson frowned. *How long does it take to find a granola bar?*

"I've got some in my pack," he grunted. He handed one—peanut butter chocolate chip—to her, followed by the two-quart water bottle. He gobbled his bar almost before she had removed the wrapper from hers.

"Are you okay?" she asked.

"Yeah."

"Are you sure? You seem impatient."

"Maybe."

"Maybe what?"

"Mom," he said, avoiding her inquiring eyes. "It's just ..."

She waited. "Just what?"

"We don't have time to sit around. And ... I don't know if you can do it."

"Do what?"

"Make it all the way to the top."

Garson felt angry at himself, seeing the hurt in her eyes.

When he first told her about it—that he wanted to study changes in a glacier for his sixth-grade science project—she vowed she'd do all she could to help. When she learned it required hiking to a mountaintop, she panicked. She phoned Garson's school and asked for his science teacher, Mr. Rock. She needed to hear the details from him.

"Not quite to the top," he had said. "But it's gonna be a tough hike to the glacier."

"Garson, I can only try. I thought it would be good for us to enjoy this together. We seldom get to share time like this."

Garson felt his stomach clench.

It was already mid-September. He needed to climb to the glacier before snow blanketed the ground. Snow could come any day up there as summer turned to fall. But he also hated himself for feeling annoyed with his mom. And for what he said to her.

Garson looked at the ground. His feelings were all mixed up, swirling around like a whirlwind. It wasn't his mom's fault. Unlike his dad, she was raised in the city. She hadn't done stuff like this before. *If only dad were here. He'd hike up the mountain with me. No problem. He's a Marine.*

"Sorry, Mom. It's just that the rest of the hike is gonna be hard."

She remained quiet, her eyes on the lake.

He pulled the topographic map from his pack and spread it across his lap.

"Look. Here's where we are." He pointed to the oblong blue splotch labeled Lupine Lake. "And here's where we started." He pointed to the end of the road where they'd begun their hike.

"That's one and a half miles."

"So, we've done pretty good," she said, trying her best to be upbeat.

"Yeah, pretty good if we were only going this far. But this is where I need to go."

Garson traced his finger across the map through the green-shaded area beyond the lake, through a band of tan beyond to a blob of pure white. In blue letters across the white were the words "Shining Mountain Glacier."

"See, it's a lot farther from here to the glacier than we've come so far." Garson looked at his mom for a reaction. He saw none.

"But more important, these brown elevation lines show how steep the mountain is," he continued. "Where the lines get closer together means it's steeper."

His mom looked closer. She traced the space between the lake and glacier with her finger. "The lines are much closer after the lake," she frowned and looked up. Her eyes fixed on the forested mountainside beyond the lake.

"Yeah, it's steeper. And there's no more trail past the lake."

Confused, the lines across her forehead pinched tighter, like the ones on the map. "No trail? Of course, there is. I saw it on the other map, the one Mr. Rock made when he did his research on the glacier."

"Oh, you're right. But it's not like the one we followed here." Garson tugged the Ziploc bag from his pack. He removed and unfolded the second map, an enlarged version of the U.S. Geological Survey topographic map. Lots of hand-written symbols and notes were jotted on it.

"We're right here, at the east end of Lupine Lake. This penciled line," Garson traced it with his finger, "is the route he told me to take from the other end of Lupine Lake to the glacier."

"So that's the trail," she reiterated, "that Mr. Rock used when he went to the glacier."

"I guess. It's just not a Forest Service trail. More of a game trail that he followed."

He looked back at his mom. She was slowly shaking her head.

"You didn't tell me it wasn't an *official* trail. One maintained by *people*, not deer."

Garson looked down at the map, mouth scrunched and lips twisted to one side. "I know. I thought if I did you wouldn't let me hike there. Then I couldn't do this project."

She studied her son before she spoke. "I know how much this means to you. But I didn't know where you were going would be so difficult, and dangerous. I should've asked your teacher more about it."

"It's not dangerous, just a long hike," he said, trying to hide his guilt while reassuring her. "Once I get there it won't take long to do the measurements and take the pictures. After that, hiking down will be a cinch."

"Not alone. I'm coming with you," she insisted.

Chapter 3
Buddy and Oreo

One Day Earlier

Buddy, a kid mountain goat, snuggled against her adopted mother, Oreo. When Oreo had found her, Buddy was desperately weak and hungry. Only three days old and without a mother, Buddy's life was surely saved by Oreo. Having just lost her own baby, Oreo found a kid in need of a mother, and Buddy found a mother in need of a kid.

Now, three months later, they were bedded atop a pile of gray, granite boulders. In a nearby melting snowdrift, Oreo had been cleansing the gash in her left shoulder. The wound she suffered, while fending off a bear intent on making a meal of Buddy, had more than crippled her. The scuffle had separated Oreo from Buddy the first day after leaving their distant home. As a result, the two goats were faced with completing their harrowing journey to Shining Mountain each on their own.

Against all odds, Buddy had made it to Shining Mountain, although not without some help from Whodare, an intrepid pygmy owl. Still more improbable, Oreo had limped there and found Buddy by following her scent. In the three following weeks, they'd become closer than ever.

Far above them, an angry mass of clouds swallowed the mountain's snow and ice-bound summit. To the south, the clouds thinned, revealing Goat Mountain's crescent-shaped bastion jutting into the sky. There, the rest of their band of goats remained. When Buddy and Oreo struck out last month, they journeyed to a place where none of their band had ever gone. Their quest—to find a new home.

For Buddy, the motive ran deeper—a driving desire to fulfill her destiny. A destiny foretold in the ancient Legend of Shining Mountain. Skeptical at first, Oreo gradually became convinced. Buddy was *called* to save the Goat Mountain band from unseen forces changing their ancestral home.

"We must think about returning to our band. I sense the seasons changing. Soon snow will be in the air," Oreo said as her gray tongue stroked Buddy's face. "I'm eager to get back to my mother and the rest of the band. Spirit was not well when we left. At thirteen, she's very old and growing feeble. Now that she has passed the mantle of matriarch to me, I must go as soon as I'm able. What good is a leader who's not with her band?"

"What about your shoulder? Can you travel that far?"

"Not yet, but soon," the nanny's voice betrayed her anxiousness. "If we wait too long, plowing through the snow will be worse than leaving before I'm fully healed."

"If we wait for the snows, maybe Ursidarr will be sleeping in her den. I don't ever want to see that bear again," Buddy quipped.

"Nor do I, little one. She has tasted enough of me."

Buddy brushed her nose against Oreo's beard. After they'd nuzzled a bit, Buddy's eyes blinked open, and she announced, "Before we go, I need to do something."

"Oh?"

"I should explore the mountain some more."

"You've already been around the summit and found it's a good place for the band."

"Yes, in summer. But you told me that everything will be buried under snow in winter. I should look for a place where the band can go in winter."

Oreo was amazed at how devoted Buddy was to the band. "You're right. But it won't be like Goat Mountain, where our winter cliffs are on the south side of the mountain. When we traveled here, we found nothing but forest on the south side of Shining Mountain. This band must winter on cliffs to the west, on the far side of the mountain. The afternoon sun will melt the snow there."

"That's what I thought you'd say. I sure wish you could go with me."

"So do I," Oreo sighed and gave Buddy's ear a tender lick. "But I better let my shoulder heal and save my strength. I'll need it for our return to Goat Mountain."

The night brought a drenching rain. Their dense summer coats insulated them; yet their sleek, ivory fur was hardly waterproof. Thankful when the sun's rays flashed above the mountain, they rose and shook the water from their coats. Sunshine did the rest.

In another month, Buddy would be fully weaned, no longer supplementing her plant diet with Oreo's milk. She didn't miss a chance to nurse before she left.

"I'll be back in one sleep," she assured Oreo.

"Watch out for Gulo. Tenanmouw may not be nearby if you run into the wolverine again."

After some final nuzzling, Buddy set off. She certainly hoped she'd come across Tenanmouw, the big billy from the band of goats who lived on Shining Mountain. If it hadn't been for him, Gulo would have eaten her the first time she explored the mountain.

The fastest way to the west side would have been around

the mountain's south slope. Nearly three hours, she guessed. Instead, Buddy headed north in hopes of stumbling on Tenanmouw. She'd found him there before.

As she ambled up the slope, the last clumps of krumholtz—whitebark pine and subalpine fir trees stunted by winter's blistering winds and suffocating snow—fell behind her. The treeless alpine meadow sprawling beyond was studded with granite rocks and boulders, like a colossal obstacle course. But for a mountain goat, this was easy going ... a walk in the park.

Ground-hugging plants filled almost every pocket of soil among the rocks. Most, however, had withered to a straw-colored patchwork. Only splashes of tasty green sprigs spattered it here and there. Bright flowers of white and yellow, ruby red and purple had dried and disappeared, but their summer fragrances remained locked in Buddy's memory bank.

She angled upward to her right. The curve of the mountain soon hid Oreo. A pang of emptiness stung her—the one Buddy felt whenever they were apart.

Shafts of sunlight splintered the morning's cloud bank. Above her shimmered the mountain's immense white dome. Focusing on the task ahead, she pushed higher.

From somewhere in the distance, a familiar call reached her. "Eeeeese!"

Her heart rate quickened. *There's no way. He wouldn't, he couldn't, travel here from Goat Mountain. But it sure sounds like Maurice!*

On the third morning of her life, after her mother had disappeared, Maurice became her first friend. He had even given Buddy her name. Hearing this shrill whistle, "Eeeeese," she realized how much she missed him. She laughed remembering when he told her how his parents named him. "Because I was a ginormous whistler, they named me "Maur-eeeese."

She squinted but couldn't spot a marmot. She scanned for others, maybe members of the Shining Mountain goat band. Ones she met the day that she and Oreo arrived. The matriarch, Mystic, had accepted Buddy only after Tenanmouw had intervened. "This little goat is welcome among us," he said. "See that she's treated well."

His behavior dumbfounded the band's members. Old billies like Tenanmouw didn't treat young goats as equals. And surely not kids. Kids were lowest in the pecking order among the goats. And this kid was a total stranger to the band.

As unexpectedly as she had emerged from the forest, the strict social order of their society was turned upside down. How could this be? Only Buddy and Tenanmouw knew the answer. No other knew their secret, except Oreo, of course. With her, Buddy shared everything.

Since their arrival, Oreo and Buddy had only seen those goats once or twice. That was fine with Oreo. She remained uneasy about lingering on another band's mountain.

Because Oreo's injury kept her from traveling far, Buddy had stayed near her on the east slope of Shining Mountain, far beneath the glacier. Then, three days after they arrived, Buddy climbed alone to the glacier and followed its lower edge around the mountain. There she'd found Tenanmouw.

Now, three weeks later, Buddy reached the glacier again. It was mid-morning. She'd seen no other goats.

I'd sure like to find Tenanmouw, she mused. *He could show me where his band winters. And I'd feel a lot safer with him.*

Chapter 4
Deep Freeze

Sunlight danced across gurgling strands seeping from the glacier's margin. It reminded her of the rivulet she crossed the morning she climbed up the mountainside from the ledge where she was born. It was the June morning her mother vanished. Her desperate search to find her mom nearly cost her life. Luckily, with Maurice's help, the search led her to Oreo and the Goat Mountain band.

Still, her heart longed for her mom.

Above, Buddy could see patches of ice exposed by summer's solar heat. Still, the glacier remained mostly buried under snow. When she climbed onto it, the snow felt sooooo good on the spongy soles of her feet. She leaped and whirled and tossed her head from side to side. Coming upon a snowfield always made her frisky. After taking a bite of the frozen delight, she flopped on her side, wriggled back and forth, and shouted, "Yahoo."

The alpine air carried her shout down the mountain to unseen ears. Ears that twisted toward the sound. Ears that recognized the dinner bell.

Many times, she'd played and shouted like this on the snowfield below Goat Mountain. She was in the company of other goats there. Numbers offered security. Now she suddenly felt foolish and anxious. *Anything wanting to eat a kid goat could hear me.*

A raven circled overhead. It squawked a sharp alarm. In her experience, the most dreaded of alarms.

She bounced back to her feet. Farther up the glacier, shadows marked gaping crevasses.

"Be careful," Tenanmouw had warned her the night they slept not far from this place. "Those open cracks slice deep into the ice. Fall in and you won't get out." She shuddered, imagining icy blue slots waiting to swallow her.

Buddy's head swiveled left and right. From the corner of her eye, she caught motion below the glacier. She whirled to face it.

"Oh no," she gasped. She recognized the beast immediately. And it was bounding straight toward her.

The hair prickled along her back. Every muscle fiber twitched and sprung to high alert. Her eyes darted wildly, seeking something to climb. There was nothing. Only snow and ice above her and a rock-strewn meadow below. Not even a convenient boulder to scale.

The stocky brown animal had a bushy tail. The tail was a giveaway. This was not Ursidarr venturing high above her forest home. Up the meadow bounded the wolverine.

At thirty pounds, Buddy weighed as much as him. Problem was that the two-inch horns atop her head couldn't match Gulo's claws and those wicked teeth gleaming in his gaping mouth.

If mountain goats have nightmares, this would be the worst of them. She had to get away.

Instinct took over. Buddy clambered up the glacier, toward waiting jaws of ice. Nowhere else could she flee.

Traction was tricky. Her split hooves and dew claws—mini hooves at the back of her feet—were big for her size and helped support her weight. But the mid-morning sun had softened the snow. With each lunge, her feet sunk in and slid, slowing her retreat.

She glanced back down the glacier. Gulo vaulted onto the snow. His big paws supported him like snowshoes. Five curved claws on each provided super traction. He was gaining on her.

He wants to eat me!

As she reached the first crevasse, the wolverine was closing in. Only a few lunges away. His snarls were terrifying, "Raaarr ... Raraaarrr."

Buddy lacked the momentum to leap across the icy blue abyss. Instead, she pivoted and dashed beside the crevasse. He was snarling right behind her now. She lowered her head and drove her legs forward. She braced for his bite.

Then she heard a loud snort, unlike Gulo's throaty snarls. She stole a glance behind her. Out of nowhere, another goat was in hot pursuit. From his huge body and broken horn tip, she knew who it must be ... Tenanmouw.

The wolverine stayed focused on a dinner of young goat. Completely unaware until the moment Tenanmouw lowered his ten-inch-long battle gear and swiped Gulo into the air. "Wrrrouuurr!" Buddy heard him roar.

When she spun to face the attacker head-on, the wolverine was gone. Vanished. Replaced by Tenanmouw.

Confused, looking from side to side she blurted, "Where did he go?"

"He's in the deep freeze," Tenanmouw rumbled with a twinkle in his eye.

A faint scratching and muffled bellow echoed from the crevasse.

"Down there?"

The corners of Tenanmouw's mouth curled upward, ever so slightly. "You remember what I told you about these cracks in the ice? The other time I saved you from Gulo's bite."

"You said to be careful. If I fell in, I wouldn't get out."

"I didn't give Gulo the same advice," he grinned.

The thumping in her chest began to slow. "Was he the same one? The wolverine you saved me from before?"

"Yes. Gulo's days of hunting goats are over."

Buddy scanned the unbroken span of white. "Where'd you come from? I mean, how did you know I needed help?"

"I heard a shout, 'Yahoo,' which I now know means 'A wolverine is trying to eat me!'" Tenanmouw broke into a full-throated laugh. Buddy watched his belly jiggle and joined in a goat laugh, "Baha-haha-ba-ha."

Tenanmouw's sense of timing amazed her. Twice now he'd shown up when she was in desperate need. "Thank you for saving me, again."

"You seem to need saving more than most goats. Your wandering up here is keeping me busy. On your next outing, I suggest you include that nanny, Oreo."

"I know Oreo would protect me, like she did from the bear. But she's still healing. Saving her strength for our journey back to Goat Mountain."

"A journey she'd be making on her own, if not for me," he said, looking down his snout at her, his voice turning gruffer. "So, *what* brought you here again. Did you not learn what you wanted three weeks ago?"

Buddy suddenly felt puny facing him. And of course, she was. He was seven times her size. But more often than not, her self-assurance had kept her from grasping a simple fact: she was merely a kid.

"With your help," she began softly, "I learned what a good place Shining Mountain is for goats in summer. A better place than Goat Mountain, where our food dries out earlier from lack of snowmelt. But I need to know something more because Oreo says the snows are coming soon."

"And what might that be?"

"Oreo told me how Goat Mountain is buried in snow for many sleeps. Shining Mountain must be too. It's so much higher," she gushed. "Our band travels down to winter cliffs, where I was born. And ..."

Tenanmouw gave a snort, "You want me to show you the Shining Mountain band's winter home, don't you?"

"Yes, yes that's it! Will you show me?"

The Legend Story As Told By Roark

Long, long ago, toward the end of the Great Ice Age, a Great Warming began melting snow and ice from the mountains of the West. Animals that lived in the cold either adapted to the changing conditions or they perished.

"As hardship befell both goats and ravens on Goat Mountain, two legendary heroes stepped forth—the mystical billy goat, Mouw, and Ten, the magical raven. Mouw mined rock with his horns, freeing slabs of limestone from the valleys. He heaped the rock onto Ten's broad back. Load after load, Ten winged skyward on the morning updrafts and piled the rock where Shining Mountain stands today. Soaring so high, the summit grew a dome of snow and ice. Shining Mountain became a refuge from the Great Warming. "

"But why? Why did they build it?" Buddy asked Roark in a whisper.

"Mouw and Ten foresaw times when each winter's snow melted earlier. Without the snow's meltwaters, tender, nutritious foods for goats became scarce by mid-summer. Nannies began bearing weak babies. Because the lives of ravens and goats are forever linked, together these ancient heroes built a lofty new home."

Chapter 5
The Cliffs

Saturday, September 14

Buddy followed the big billy goat off the glacier. They briskly crossed the meadow, stopping only when Tenanmouw spotted an especially tasty patch of grasses and limestone columbine. Columbine, he had told her when they were here three weeks ago, was a very important plant on Shining Mountain. "Nannies eat it so their babies are born healthy and grow strong."

Maybe that's why, Buddy reasoned, *I'm the only kid born last spring who survived ... there's not much columbine on Goat Mountain.* She furrowed her brow. *But Oreo says our band has lived on Goat Mountain for a very long time. There must be another reason why our band's numbers are shrinking.*

Her eyes locked on the lush vegetation watered by the melting glacier. *I know that Spirit and Oreo are always saying that things are changing on Goat Mountain, like the snow melting away earlier each summer. And that it's getting harder to find nutritious plants. I wonder if that's it?*

By midday, the two reached the west side of Shining Mountain. They ambled down the meadow, into drifts of krumholtz at the upper treeline. The trees' branches tangled like clasping fingers.

"Follow me," he said.

Tufts of goat fur dangled from branches along Tenanmouw's zigzagging route through the stunted trees. Emerging from the krumholtz, they picked their way through a much friendlier forest of whitebark pine and subalpine fir.

Throughout the morning, Buddy saw no members of the Shining Mountain band, and much to her relief, no more wolverines. One was enough, even with the big guy to protect her.

I'll be glad when I'm bigger like Tenanmouw. Then I'll be able to take care of myself. Only her small size did Buddy regard as a limitation.

She, of course, would never be as big as him, some 200 pounds. Nannies grew to full size when five or six years old. The very biggest ones—like Oreo or Spirit—topped out at 150 pounds. Nonetheless, with horns equal in length to those of billies, tenacious nannies could well defend themselves.

Tenanmouw spent little time with other goats, except during mating season. But he was fond of this kid from a distant mountain. She was courageous. More importantly, they shared their common calling.

As they paused for a drink from a cascade, Tenanmouw casually said, "I've heard from Roark."

Buddy's ears shot up. Roark was the messenger raven who had led Oreo to her as Buddy lay on death's doorstep. She was indebted to him. Then Roark had *chosen* her to become next in a long line of goats entrusted with safeguarding the Legend of Shining Mountain.

But Buddy sensed her destiny was more than that. More than simply keeping the Legend story alive. Her journey with Oreo to Shining Mountain was to fulfill that destiny, she believed. Roark had set her on this path. He was her friend, counselor, and counterpart.

"What did Roark say?" she asked Tenanmouw, who keenly eyed her.

"He told me that you are now the Goat Mountain band's goat-Keeper of the Legend. Battenmouw has given his consent for you to succeed him."

Despite learning this from Roark a week earlier, it somehow hadn't felt real. Now Buddy felt validated. Hearing it from Tenanmouw, the Shining Mountain band's goat-Keeper of the Legend, affirmed it.

"I truly hope at your young age you understand how great a responsibility this is," Tenanmouw added.

Buddy felt a spasm of doubt. This goat-Keeper job wasn't something she'd asked for. Yet, she hadn't said no.

Although she couldn't fully sort it out or put it into words, she unswervingly believed she had some purpose to fulfill. *There must be a reason I survived after mom disappeared.* When Buddy first confided this, Oreo simply said, "You must find how best you can contribute to the band."

She looked at Tenanmouw squarely. "I do understand. I think you know it too."

The big billy was taken aback. And this wasn't the first time her demeanor had unsettled him. "Yes, to find a new home for your band. Something the Legend foretold."

Involuntarily, Buddy stamped her front foot in frustration.

"But I think there's more."

"More? More than the safety of your band?" he huffed.

"Yes. I'm ... I'm just not sure what it is."

There was silence. Tenanmouw's gaze pierced her as if trying to penetrate her thoughts.

"I think there's a bigger message ... in the Legend. And something Mystic said makes me think that's true."

"Mystic?" Tenanmouw raised his head to its full impressive

height. "She may be the matriarch of the Shining Mountain band, but Mystic knows not of things concerning the Legend."

"When I first got here, I told Mystic that our band was in trouble. And I came here hoping Shining Mountain might be a better home for us."

"I know that. Roark told me. What's that got to do with Mystic?"

"When I told Mystic why I'd come, she said this to me. I remember her exact words, 'What affects one goat, or one band, affects us all. As where you come from, I see changes here as well.'"

Tenanmouw squinted. His glare made her take a step back. He unnerved her. Still, she had to say what had been gnawing at her.

"Maybe she's right," Buddy continued. "The Legend has a message for us all—the Goat Mountain band and the Shining Mountain band too."

Tenanmouw didn't reply. He studied this outsider from Goat Mountain. Then he turned his head to the south. On the horizon a horseshoe-shaped block of granite, crested by a thin drift of snow, shimmered in the midday sun. None of his band had ever been there. Nor had goats from that distant mountain ventured to his domain. Not until this precocious kid arrived. Yet he knew about Goat Mountain's goats, the same way Buddy knew how Shining Mountain had come to be. The Legend was the bond the two goats shared as goat-Keeper of the Legend for their respective bands. It was a lofty calling they shared with only one other: Roark, the raven-Keeper.

Tenanmouw chose to ignore Mystic's words of warning to Buddy, at least for now. He turned and ambled down the slope. Over his shoulder, he said, "The winter cliffs are ahead."

When Buddy caught up, the big billy had halted. The mountain fell away below them in a jumble of cliffs, gullies, and spires. Ledges sparsely dotted with trees and low-growing plants creased the cliffs. On one ledge, Buddy spotted three white specs. Farther south, several more navigated a knife-edged ridge. Tenanmouw was looking at them too.

"I see some of the band, including Mystic, have felt the draw to our winter home."

The steep, broken mountainside continued to their left and right. It all plunged thousands of feet and out of sight to a faint rumble below. For a moment she felt lightheaded. Then an amazing warmth flushed her body. For her small band of goats, waiting back on Goat Mountain, this would be a fine winter home.

"This is like where I was born, only bigger. These cliffs must be a safe place for your band in winter."

Charmed by her passion, Tenanmouw nodded, "You have a fine sense of what goats need, despite not living through a winter yourself. That nanny taught you well."

For an awkward moment, Buddy fought the urge to nuzzle him. Instead, she said, "I'm ready to go back now."

"Back where?" he grunted.

"Back to Oreo. I can hardly wait to tell her about what you showed me."

Tenanmouw continued looking toward the white specs moving through the cliffs. Showing no indication he'd accompany her, Buddy asked, "Are you, I mean, will you go back with me?"

Tenanmouw seemed lost in thought. He replied vaguely, "No."

"I thought you might." She couldn't hide her disappointment. "There might still be a wolverine out there."

"Hrrrumph," he snorted. "Gulo's no more than a frozen block of fur."

"But what if there's another one?"

"Wolverines are loners. They stay clear of each other. There's not another one on the mountain now." Staring into the canyon's void he added, "Besides, I need to find Mystic. I need to talk to her about something you said."

Buddy cleared a lump in her throat. Her heart began to race. *Maybe I said something I shouldn't have.*

"Well," she paused, "thanks for showing me where your band winters."

With that, she turned and began plodding up the mountain. When she looked back, Tenanmouw remained fixed, staring down the cliffs.

It would be a long and lonely trek back to Oreo.

Chapter 6
End of the Trail

Garson knew better. When his mom made up her mind, it was best not to argue. Yup, she was going with him.

"Okay. Then we outta get started," he said, rising from the driftwood log where they had eaten a snack. Slipping his arms through the pack straps, he added, "Alright if I lead?"

"Of course."

Garson intended to set a faster pace, faster than on the hike to the lake. Otherwise, he might run out of daylight on the way back down the mountain. Even though he had a flashlight, he sure didn't want to hike in the dark.

Besides, he was pretty sure of one thing. Although his mom insisted she was going with him, he'd be hiking to the summit alone. And the longer he was gone, the more she'd worry.

The trail followed the lake, a sapphire blue gash in the forested basin. Not a breath of breeze sighed through the pines. Fallen needles muffled their footfalls. Their progress was silent until ...

"Oh Garson, look at these pretty flowers. I think they're daisies."

He wanted to keep hiking. Pretend he didn't hear her. Instead, he stopped and watched her snapping shots with her phone and pick a small bunch. He wanted to shout, "We don't have time for pictures," but he didn't.

"Sorry, but they're such a pretty lavender. I wanted a picture to remember our hike."

"Yeah, they're pretty, Mom," Garson replied. He snapped a photo of her and added, "There's probably lots more further up the mountain."

While his mom ambled with her eyes peeled for trailside flowers, Garson's eyes fixed on the mountain and sky ahead.

The lake was a quarter-mile long, a five-minute hike. It took them fifteen. At the end of the lake, the spruce, firs, and lodgepole pines gave way to a little meadow. In the middle was a fire ring. It hadn't been used for a while. Garson looked for any sign of a path leading up the forested slope to the west.

"Oh, this is pretty," his mother said when she caught up with him. "But which way do we go from here?"

"This is the end of the hiking trail. But I think I found the game trail Mr. Rock said goes up the mountain." He pointed to a faint path disappearing into the trees. "It's pretty crude."

He read the look on her face. *You've gotta be kidding me,* she thought.

Without pausing further, he began trudging up the mountain. Trees and low shrubs clutched the path. Still wet from last night's rain, the soil was studded with deer tracks.

They hadn't gone far when his mom called out, "Wait, I can't go this fast."

He heard her wheezing. Alarmed she was struggling to breathe, he scrambled back to her.

"Mom," he exclaimed.

He'd seen her have an asthma attack before. It frightened him, wondering if she might stop breathing. That was at home. Up here, far from the car and much farther from medical care, an attack could be dangerous. How dangerous he wasn't sure.

"It's alright. I ... I gotta ... catch my breath."

Twice she inhaled from the puffer and tucked it back into her pullover pocket.

Garson didn't like the panic he saw in her eyes. He suddenly felt queasy.

"Let's go back down to the lake. To the meadow, until you feel better."

"I'll be fine," she wheezed with her hands on her knees. "I'm just not used to climbing straight up a mountain."

He took her hand and led her down the game trail. When they reached the meadow, he helped her sit down. She clutched her legs to her chest and slightly rocked forward and back. Garson knelt beside her.

"Mom, I'm worried about you."

"I'll be okay."

"It's still a long way to the top. And the climb is going to get worse."

"But you need to go up there ... for your project," she rasped.

"I know. But I think this is gonna be too hard for you." Garson hesitated. He softly added, "I think I should go to the glacier on my own."

Mrs. Strangewalker was silent. She gazed at the lake. Between the rings fashioned by rising fish, its tranquil surface reflected the cheerless forest. The thought of Garson climbing up the mountain on his own, to a place he'd never been, terrified her. It went against her deepest instincts to protect her son. Oddly, a parallel reaction nudged her. She had not seen this determination, this sense of purpose in Garson.

She had wanted him to ask a friend to join them today. Someone in his class. Someone who was a strong hiker, in case she couldn't do it. In case her asthma foiled her best efforts. But Garson hadn't.

"Maybe someone else can go with you on another weekend,"

she probed, hoping the suggestion wouldn't disappoint him.

"Why? We're already here. I've gotta do this before snow comes. That could be any day up there," his voice becoming more strident as he spoke.

Mrs. Strangewalker felt her heart racing. There seemed to be no way out of this dilemma. Climbing up the mountain she knew would be impossible for her. She was frightened of having an asthma attack up here. And she couldn't bear letting Garson go on his own. She would never forgive herself if something happened to him. Either way, she'd fail him.

Something caught her attention. An eagle, brilliant white head and tail bookending its stout brown body, glided over the lake, all alone. Her heart had slowed. Her breathing returned to near normal. She suddenly felt a calm sweep over her as the eagle's legs plunged into the lake's waters. Beating its wings until freed from the water's surface, it lifted into the still air, clutching a fish in its talons. Rising powerfully, it screeched as if in triumph.

She looked at Garson and exclaimed, "Did you see that?"

"Yeah, really cool!" He grinned as his eyes tracked the eagle winging away with its catch of the day held fast beneath.

She allowed herself the thought of letting her son climb the mountain alone. She knew he was capable. Although slender-built, Garson was strong. He had the speed and endurance to be on his school's track and cross-country teams. But despite her encouragement, he didn't try out. Something held him back. He wasn't competitive by nature. She also knew he wasn't brimming with self-confidence, which was why he wasn't especially social. He preferred spending time in the woods near their house, running along forest trails, alone. Or, more recently, in his room reading about glaciers.

Since his father had been gone, he'd become introverted and

quiet. Not that he was ever an outgoing kid. His enthusiasm about school this year was therefore surprising but heartening to Lucy. It gratified her to see him impassioned. It surely eased her anxiety about her only child.

I have to let him go, she thought.

"How long will it take? I mean, how long before you'll be back down here?" she asked hesitantly.

He looked at her, half shocked. Recovering, he scrunched his mouth, his lips twisted to one side. Mr. Rock had said it could take two or three hours to get to the Glacier, but Garson really didn't know if he'd be that fast, or how long everything would take. He did know this. If he exaggerated how quickly he could hike there, do his work and return, she'd worry if he took longer. He pulled out the map Mr. Rock gave him. He squinted at the contour lines indicating the route's steepness. He could only assume the game trail would continue through the forest to the alpine meadow above.

"It's almost ten o'clock. I'll be back at the car by five."

"Five? That's seven hours. Are you sure?"

"Not really," he said, averting his eyes, "but I don't want to say less and make you worry."

"I'll worry if you're gone half as long."

"I know, Mom. But the glacier's still over two thousand feet of elevation up. I really think it might take me that long."

She lowered her eyes to the map spread across his lap. Garson thought she was about to change her mind.

"I can do this. Thanks for trusting me."

She threw her arms around him and blinked the tears from her eyes, fighting hard to keep her emotions from exploding. She leaned back and held his face between her hands.

"Okay. You best get going. But if it's going to take that long, you'll need plenty of food and water. Here." She rummaged in her daypack. "Take my lunch and top off your water bottle with some of mine."

"I'll be okay, you keep it."

"No, I insist. I've got more at the car if I need it."

Garson knew she never left the house without a bottle of water and some snacks in the car. "In case of an emergency," she always said.

How could there be an emergency going to the store, he wondered, *or to work, or ...?* It's how she was, and now he was glad those "emergency" things were in the car.

With food and water transferred, he grabbed a pack strap and rose to his feet. He gave his mom a hand up.

"I'll wait for you at the car," she said.

Garson nodded his head yes.

"One more thing, take my phone."

Mrs. Strangewalker was never without her phone, always keeping it handy. Not Garson. He never asked his mother for a phone. He didn't want one, even though most kids in his class had one. Garson thought his classmates looked like electronically controlled zombies, constantly eyeballing their phones—except while in class where students were forbidden to have them turned on, or visible—sometimes bumping into each other while walking the halls. He called it their "three by five stare."

That only added to other kids treating him like an oddball. Strangewalker, the weirdo who had no one to call.

Placing the cased phone in his hand she said, "This is a new phone I just got a couple days ago."

A puzzled look crossed Garson's face. "I didn't know you had a new phone. Did the old one quit working?"

"This one has better technology and a new number. I left my old phone in the car. It's still active with the old number. The one you know."

"You might need it. You still have to hike back to the car," he muttered.

"I'll be fine." She took his hand. "Be sure to call me when you get up there. Or if you should ..." She caught herself imagining the worst.

"Okay, but there might not be any cell service up there."

A shiver of fear shook her. Could she change her mind? *No, I need to let go. I need to trust him.* "If you can't reach me, then try Mr. Rock or Amanda. Their numbers are in the contacts list. I also wrote both their numbers on a piece of paper that's in the case."

She didn't mention that she'd also written down the sheriff's office number. He'd see it.

They stood silently looking at each other. Garson considering how she thought of every possibility that might arise; she feeling that she'd just made one of the biggest decisions of her life.

She heaved a sigh. "Okay. I'll see you back at the car. Please be careful. Please." She hugged him so hard he wondered if she'd let go.

Releasing her grip, she backed away. With trembling lips, she said, "I love you."

"I love you too."

He shoved his arm through the other pack strap and set off toward the forest. After a few steps, he stopped and turned back. "You're the best, Mom."

She gave a wave as he vanished into the trees.

Chapter 7

The Climb

The scent of pines and damp soil hung heavy on the forest air. Garson breathed it in and relished the feeling of exertion as his legs drove him upward. He was going to savor this challenge.

Yet, thoughts about his mother preoccupied him. Was he wrong in leaving her to return to the car on her own? Would her asthma plague her? Had he been selfish to insist he climb to the glacier alone, knowing she'd worry about him? It wasn't her fault he didn't have a dad to do outdoor things with him. He knew that. She did her best to serve the role of two parents.

He stopped. *Maybe I should go back.*

No. I can't. This might be my only chance before snow covers the mountain. He kicked at the dirt. *She'll be alright,* he told himself. *But I've gotta hurry.*

He hoisted the pack with its fifteen pounds of contents higher on his shoulders, grabbed the straps in front of his chest, and beat a fast pace up the game trail. His legs and lungs pumped rhythmically. The slope was steeper than any place he'd ever hiked. It felt good.

In the forest, the trail was mostly dirt. He looked for boot tracks. He saw none. *With all these trees cluttering the ground, who'd want to hike here?* He clambered over their trunks, or when they were too high or their limbs too thick, found his way around. Their upended roots, sometimes measuring fifteen feet across, glowered like whorls of giant octopus tentacles.

When the trail sometimes split, he tried to choose whichever fork headed most directly up the mountain. Other times he'd stay on the most obvious branch, the one most heavily traveled by deer or elk or whatever else might be living here.

Where animals had chosen several ways through the forest, Garson sometimes lost his way completely. He wove through the undergrowth of huckleberry, snowberry, and other shrubs searching ahead. Somehow a trail always reemerged.

Mr. Rock knew the difficulty Garson would encounter following the route. To make a bread crumb trail, he gave him two rolls of surveyor tape, "Hang a foot of this from limbs every so often. When you come back down the mountain, you can follow your markers to the lake."

As Garson marched upward, he left a trail of fluorescent pink. The fluttering signposts glowed in the forest gloom.

He stopped once to get a drink and eat half a ham and cheese sandwich. A little further, he stopped again when he heard something crash, unseen, through the forest. His heart pounded. He blinked to clear his eyes and stared into the sunlight-dappled shadows. A bead of sweat trickled down his back. Nothing. Silence returned. He released his grip from the holstered canister of pepper spray on his belt.

In the woods near his house—the place he often ran after school—he'd seen bears. But he could count the number of times on one hand and not use all the fingers. He'd never thought of it as a big deal. They livened up his jog and always ran away.

Mr. Rock encountered bears forty years ago on Shining Mountain. Bears that maybe had never seen a human. Bears perhaps without fear of two-legged intruders. He insisted Garson take precautions, particularly because he was advising

Garson on this project. He didn't want a missing student on his conscience.

Mr. Rock had purchased a canister of bear repellant; what everyone called pepper spray. He'd shown Garson how to use it the day he taught him to orienteer with map and compass. Made him practice using it ... more than once.

"Take it with you to Shining Mountain," he said. "Better safe than sorry."

When Garson answered his mom's question about the holstered canister on his belt, it's fair to say she freaked out. "Bears? There are bears up there?"

"Probably not. Mr. Rock wanted me to take it as a precaution. You know, like carrying a band-aid in case you cut a finger," Garson had said rather cleverly, he thought.

Other than the protection on his belt, which felt welcome despite its weight, he planned to carry no more than necessary to travel fast. His pack contained high-energy, lightweight foods, a simple first-aid kit, his bird field guide, a pen, and a spiral notebook. A single two-quart bottle of water would be enough. He could refill it from the glacier's meltwaters.

Mr. Rock had loaned him all the necessary equipment: the map, compass, and altimeter to orienteer plus a laser rangefinder to measure distances. He really liked the sound of the word, altimeter. Finally, he could test his orienteering skills on Shining Mountain, well beyond the local park where Mr. Rock had trained him. He carried a GPS unit. With it, he'd enter waypoints for each reference point that Mr. Rock had established back in the dark ages before GPS.

Another essential item was a 35mm Nikkormat camera with two 36-exposure rolls of Ektachrome 100 slide film, one loaded in the camera and a spare. In case. For reference, Garson packed 8x10 photocopies of Mr. Rock's original photos in the

Ziploc with the map.

The camera was kind of heavy, but Mr. Rock thought it best to use the same camera he had used. The format and quality of Garson's photos would match the forty-year-old images. Besides, Garson didn't own a camera.

To save weight, he bought a collapsible tripod at a second-hand store, rather than lug the bulky one Mr. Rock had used. It saved at least two pounds.

The repeat photos he'd take would create a visual record of changes in the glacier over time. Mr. Rock was certain it had shrunk. But how much? That was Garson's mystery to solve. Sometimes when he thought about the significance of it, the hair on his neck prickled.

The other item always with him—whether hiking, running, eating, or sleeping—was in his front pocket. Whenever he felt unsure or afraid, but also excited, he clutched and rubbed his thumb across its surface. The shiny red Swiss Army knife was his security crutch and rabbit's foot rolled into one. His father had given it to him before leaving for Afghanistan. Inlaid in silver were the words, "Garson from Dad."

Garson was strong. Moreover, when it came to this project, he was determined. As he trudged up the mountain, following one thread of trail into obscurity until he found another, sweat soaked his back. Twice more he heard branches breaking in the forest. He involuntarily grasped the pepper spray on his waist. Once he saw the white flash of a mule deer's rump, saving his imagination from conjuring up some beast with large, pointy teeth. Besides bears, there could be mountain lions here. Of course, a lion would remain as quiet as dew forming on leaves. They were the stealth hunters of the forest.

After nearly two hours of climbing, the dense growth of spruce and firs thinned. Trees grew shorter. He noticed a new kind of tree now predominated over the others. Whitebark pine. This conifer grew at the highest elevations that trees could live. Higher up, only low-growing shrubs and non-woody plants could survive the howling winds and smothering snows of six-month winters.

Weaving through the pines, he no longer needed a trail. One foot in front of the other now, up and up. To know where to enter the forest on his return, he tied more pink flags to branches. These fluttering guideposts would lead him back to Lupine Lake.

When he broke from the last pines, patches of krumholtz striped the open slope. These four-foot-high remnants of conifer forest ended maybe another 300 feet higher. An ankle-high meadow, turned golden-brown by freezing nights and dry summer weather, rolled beyond. Gray and silver rocks, most covered in black, gray, pale green, and dazzling orange lichens, flecked the meadow in a painted landscape like Garson had never seen. He stopped to snap a couple of pictures and took a GPS reading of the elevation. *I wonder if the treeline is different from when Mr. Rock was here forty years ago?*

After gulping more water, he hoisted his pack. As he wove through the krumholtz then trudged up the meadow, an awesome sight slowly broke the horizon. A mantle of white shimmered beneath an azure sky. Garson was awed by its beauty.

Chapter 8
Mr. Rock

At Lupine Lake, Mrs. Strangewalker sat near the shore, nervously glancing over her shoulder. She fondled the canister of bear repellant that Garson pulled from his pack and gave her before leaving.

How thoughtful. Was it Garson's doing, or did Mr. Rock suggest he bring two of those on their hike? Probably the latter, she guessed. She was grateful, nonetheless.

His science teacher was having a positive influence on her son. In some small way, he was filling the space left by the absence of Garson's father. She felt tears welling. She wiped them away, trying to focus on the lake's mirrored surface, but glad she couldn't see the reddened eyes and lines in her face.

A bald eagle set its wings, extended its talons, and snatched a fish. Of all the dimples from rising fish, the eagle picked one. *It chose that one,* she thought. *Of all the students at the Chief Joseph School, Garson is the one Mr. Rock had taken a special interest in this summer. The one he trusted to repeat his research from years ago.*

This had made an indelible impression on her son. She recalled Garson's eagerness, whenever she asked, to tell her about those Saturdays spent with Mr. Rock. And even when she didn't ask.

A rustling in the trees behind her halted her thoughts. She

rolled onto her knees, pointing the canister of repellant in outstretched arms. *What's that?*

Snap!

Her heart thumped in her chest. Both hands squeezed the canister.

A mule deer stepped into the meadow, followed by a pale-spotted fawn. A tense smile of relief creased Mrs. Strangewalker's face as she exhaled an audible breath.

At the sound, the doe's head jerked to attention. Both deer sniffed the air, whirled, and bolted into the trees. Seeing her trembling hands, she shook her head. She hadn't slid the safety off the canister to arm her defense.

Her mind drifted to her husband. *I'm not meant to be an outdoorsman, not like John. As if I didn't already know that.*

She slipped her belt through the repellant's holster loop and rose. *Time I got back to the car.* She hit the trail at a steady pace.

During the forty-five minutes of walking, her thoughts returned to last spring's arts and science festival. The kids presenting projects at the festival were sixth graders and older, with dedicated classroom science teachers. Garson's fifth grade had a limited science curriculum, so he wasn't eligible to participate, even if he had wanted to. Still, the festival was a turning point in her son's life.

Garson knew little about the festival. She remembered him grumbling "it's probably an auditorium stuffed with nerdy kids and parents bragging about ... who knows what." He wasn't interested to find out.

"Why don't you come with me?" his mom had asked. "It could be fun to see what the students have done."

"Naw, doesn't sound like fun to me. Why're you goin' there anyway?"

"I thought I told you. I'm producing a piece about the fair for the TV station."

Garson vaguely recalled.

"I'll take you out for pizza afterward," she slyly added.

Pizza. Reflexively, his mouth watered.

"I guess, as long as we don't have to stay long. Probably all there'll be is guppies in fishbowls and blinking robots."

He tagged along with his mom at first as she interviewed students. Their projects were stapled to poster boards arranged on tables. A cameraman and sound guy had met her there.

"I'm gonna walk around," he said.

After acknowledging with a weak wave to him, his mom turned back to a girl with a microscope naming the small creatures in an aquarium of pond water.

The school auditorium was alive with chatter. Garson was impressed by how many people, parents, kids, and student presenters, had turned out. Impressed, alright, but not in a positive way. He hated crowds.

Maybe someone's done a bird project, he thought as he began to wander. He hadn't gone far when a girl with freckles and wavy red hair exclaimed, "Get ready. Here it goes!"

"Vulcanism" the poster beside her was titled. On the table was a two-foot-high cone with a hollow top. By mixing water, dish soap, and vinegar with baking soda in a bottle she slipped into its open back, the paper mâché volcano spouted a stream of red magma—thanks to red food coloring. What caught Garson's attention wasn't the spouting slurry of goo, but something else.

"What's that supposed to be?" Garson asked, pointing to the white splotch covering one side of the gray summit.

"It's a glacier," Kira, the student responsible for the impressive mess oozing onto the table told him.

Garson frowned, "How can something as cold as a glacier be

on a volcano with magma inside?"

The student couldn't answer Garson's question, but her science teacher overheard their exchange.

"Lots of volcanoes have glaciers," smiled Mr. Rock. "Mostly inactive ones."

Gauging the puzzled look on the boy's face, Mr. Rock added, "If you're really interested, I suggest you pick up a copy of *Glaciers of the World* to learn about it. It's in the school library. Give me a call if you have any questions after reading it."

Garson was over the moon. Mr. Rock, who'd be Garson's science teacher next fall, said he could call him. It made him somehow feel ... important. Because Garson rarely read anything not required, his mom was shocked when he came home the next week with *Glaciers of the World.*

Garson loved the book. He kept it on the nightstand beside his bed. He read and reread it, pouring over the pictures. He went to sleep and dreamed about glaciers. He woke up thinking about glistening fields of ice covering Kilimanjaro, Mount Blanc, Everest, Denali, and other high peaks.

Other than Antarctica and Greenland, which are mostly covered by massive ice sheets, ice is a rare feature across the Earth's land surface, Garson learned. Excluding the ice sheets, which hardly anyone sees, only about half a percent of the Earth's land surface is covered by the remaining ice. What geologists call glaciers.

After the school librarian politely told him he couldn't continue renewing *Glaciers of the World*, his mom bought Garson a copy. At the town's public library, Garson found other books about glaciers. One at a time, he checked them out. The photos fascinated him, especially the ones retaken over time. They showed, without a doubt, how glaciers were shrinking.

At the dinner table, he rattled off facts each evening.

"There are glaciers on every continent, except Australia. Most of them have been around for hundreds of thousands, maybe millions of years. And you know what else?"

Mrs. Strangewalker's fork and knife hovered over her plate. Her son's enthusiasm was infectious. "What else?"

"The ice in glaciers is so thick and heavy it actually moves ... like something living. Not that people can actually see them crawling." Garson poked some peas across his plate. "Scientists learned it by studying them for years."

Garson paused and examined his mom. "Don't you think it's awful?"

"Think what's awful?"

"Something so big and old could actually disappear?"

She laid her silverware down. Elbows on the table, hands folded beneath her chin, she eyed him intently. *I haven't seen this much passion in him since we took the training wheels off his bike.*

"They think some might not disappear ... only shrink a lot. Then the glaciologists won't call what's left glaciers. Just ice and snowfields. Do you think those could disappear too?"

Without waiting for an answer, Garson continued, "This one scientist has studied the ones in Glacier National Park since 1991. Guess what he thinks?"

"I don't know."

"He thinks the park's glaciers might be gone by 2030. All of them gone in a few years!"

"How does he know?"

"Because of how fast they're getting smaller."

"Really?"

"Yeah. There's this one amazing website I found. Its pictures show the park's glaciers disappearing. There were about 150 glaciers in 1850 when the park was first explored. Now only 25 are left. All the rest are gone!"

Garson pursed his lips and scrunched his forehead. "I wonder if Shining Mountain, the one we can see from the other side of town, has a glacier?"

"Why not look it up?"

"Where?"

"Maybe try Google Earth."

As he helped his mom clear the dinner table, Garson rattled off more facts he'd learned. He posed more questions she had no idea how to answer.

"I'll finish up the dishes. Go ahead and see what you can find out about that mountain."

Garson pulled up a Google Earth map of the mountain range west of his home. Sure enough, on the pyramid-shaped summit of the range's highest peak rested a giant scoop of vanilla ice cream. The Shining Mountain Glacier. He bounded downstairs.

Garson found his mother studying production notes for an upcoming segment on health care for the TV station. She looked up and saw him grinning.

"Guess what I found?"

After telling her, he added, "I wonder if Mr. Rock knows about this? I wonder if he knows about what's happening to that glacier?"

"Why not ask him?" she replied.

Chapter 9

Shining Mountain

It was a Thursday in early August, three months after the school's spring arts and science festival. In the phone book, Garson found a single entry under the last name Rock—D. Rock. Nervously, he punched the number sequence on the phone.

"Hello."

"Mr. Rock?"

"Yes."

"This is Garson, the boy you talked to at the festival last spring." Pause. "About glaciers."

Pause on the other end.

"I read the book you told me about, *Glaciers of the World*."

"Oh yes." An image of a thin boy with a mop of brown hair and probing brown eyes formed in his mind. The boy's uncommon curiosity is what he remembered most.

"What did you think about it?"

"It was the best. And I read more stuff about glaciers too."

Garson couldn't see the smile on Mr. Rock's face. It was so seldom a student took the initiative to do something like this during summer break, much less when it was something this dear to Mr. Rock's heart.

"I've got a question," Garson said with some hesitation.

"Go ahead. Shoot."

"Do you know about the glacier on Shining Mountain?"

The boy's question broadened the teacher's smile. "Actually, I do. I spent some time up there."

"You did?"

Garson's excitement leapt through the phone.

"That was many years ago, though I remember those days well."

"Are you going up there again?"

"Why do you ask?"

"Well ... if you were ..."

Mr. Rock could hear the boy's question without the words being spoken.

"You may not know this, but before I became a teacher, I studied glaciers. I still have a special interest in them. It sounds like you do too."

"Yeah."

"Shining Mountain is perhaps my favorite glacier of all."

"Really? Why?"

"How about I show you why."

"Would you?!"

"If it's okay with your parents, we could meet and talk about it."

"Really?"

"Sure. How about Saturday at the school's soccer field, say at eleven o'clock."

"Gee thanks."

Garson's hand instinctively found the Swiss Army knife in his pocket. He rubbed it in his fingers. "I'll ask my mom and call you right back."

Mrs. Strangewalker agreed. "You can go on Saturday, on one condition. I'll drive you there," she insisted.

"But mom, I can ride my bike. You don't need to take me."

"I know, but I'd like to meet Mr. Rock too."

After some back and forth, Mrs. Strangewalker said Garson could put his bike in the Subaru. When he was done talking to Mr. Rock, he could ride home.

"I'll only stay for a little while. I want to thank him for offering his time to talk to you."

Yes, she would express her gratitude. But protective mom that she was, she also wanted to learn who he was.

When they arrived on Saturday, Mr. Rock was sitting at a picnic table in the shade of a big cottonwood tree. Eleven o'clock and it was already warm. Beside him was a tan, canvas rucksack. Tattered and water-stained, it had seen plenty of use. With a toothy smile, he rose to greet them.

"Hello, I'm Lucy Strangewalker, Garson's mother."

Mr. Rock extended his hand. "Wonderful to meet you. Your son has been very busy since we met last spring. Hello, Garson," he shook Garson's hand enthusiastically.

He was an imposing man, broad-shouldered and over six-feet tall. His unruly, thinning gray hair spilled across the forehead of a kind face with lively blue eyes.

But what also struck Mrs. Strangewalker was when he walked to greet them, he limped. Not a limp from a stiff leg, but the marked hobble caused by some disability. She held her eyes on his face to avoid betraying she noticed.

"Let's sit here in the shade, where we can talk about what you've been learning about glaciers."

Garson propped his bike against the end of the table and sat next to his mom, across from Mr. Rock. Before their discussion began, Mr. Rock asked how long they'd lived in Pinewood.

"Garson and I moved here five years ago from North Carolina ... Camp LeJeune. It was a move to be near my husband's parents."

Camp LeJeune, he knew, was a Marine Corps base. There

was no Marine base anywhere near Pinewood, let alone one in this state. Maybe her husband had been discharged. He chose not to ask.

"Must be nice having your grandparents nearby," Mr. Rock said.

"They aren't anymore," Garson softly replied, his eyes falling on the rucksack beside the man.

"Shortly after we moved here," Mrs. Strangewalker clarified, "they moved to Arizona. Health reasons. Their doctor recommended it."

What could she tell him? She had no other relatives in the community. No support networks. Working and raising her son on her own had been tough, especially with the uncertainty surrounding her husband's circumstances.

"I know. Sometimes things don't work out how we expect," Mr. Rock replied in a tone suggesting he'd experienced hardship of his own.

"But we like it here," she responded, trying to make the conversation more upbeat. "We have a comfy log cabin on the west edge of town, not far from the national forest."

"Sounds nice. I like that side of town. Cooler in summer with the mountains blocking the late afternoon sun."

About then a man rode by on the bike path and shouted, "Hey Doc. Nice day for a picnic."

"And for a ride," Mr. Rock responded.

"He called you Doc," Garson said.

"He did."

"So, your name's Doc Rock," Garson blurted with a grin.

"Doc's what my friends started calling me years ago. Probably had to do with my career as a research geologist. And, of course, it rhymes," he added with a twinkle in his eye.

"But you'll call him Mr. Rock," his mother interjected.

"Hard to believe my studies of glaciers began forty years ago ... right up there on Shining Mountain. I intended to repeat the measurements I did back then to record any changes. But then the accident happened," he added, patting his leg.

"You couldn't go back to the glacier?" Garson awkwardly asked, feeling his mother's eyes burning into him.

"It's what led to my retirement from the Geological Survey. I couldn't hike up mountains to do the fieldwork anymore. I couldn't see myself riding a desk, shuffling reports and analyzing data other scientists collected. There had to be something more rewarding to do.

After my wife passed away, I took a leap of faith and moved to Pinewood." At a nearby college, he explained, he'd earned a teaching certificate. "I may hold some record as the oldest student to do that."

Then, he'd applied and was hired as Pinewood school's sixth and seventh grades science teacher. Garson and his mom had arrived a year earlier.

"But why here?" she asked.

"This town sits below maybe the prettiest piece of paradise I've ever seen. So, in my opinion, you made a good choice too."

They were silent for a minute, then he continued.

"You see," his eyes drifted upward, "I spent some of the best days of my life up there ... doing my graduate research. Like I said, I planned to go back someday. Try to find the markers I pounded into the ground. But after the accident, reality set in. Someone else would have to do it. Someone who was strong enough and interested in the science. Someone who wanted to learn what's happening to the glacier, and what it means for us."

A tingling sensation surged through Garson's body. In his pocket, he flipped the jackknife in his fingers. "No one's been back to study it?"

Mr. Rock sighed, "Not so far."

Garson glanced at his mother, who was listening as intently as Garson, and then back at Mr. Rock. Excitedly he said, "Maybe I could do it."

As his gaze passed from Garson to Mrs. Strangewalker, a wry smile crossed his face. "You know, maybe you could."

Mrs. Strangewalker felt a shiver of unease at Mr. Rock's response. She nervously glanced at her watch. "Oh, I have to leave soon. Duty calls," she quipped. "But first," she said as she pulled two plastic bags from the reusable cloth bag beside her, "lunch is served."

"Well, what an unexpected surprise," Mr. Rock thanked her.

Over a lunch of ham and cheese sandwiches, with pickles and chips on the side, Mrs. Strangewalker chatted about the adjustment moving required of them. Garson listened as she talked, hearing his life of the past five years play out. A life that left him feeling isolated and withdrawn.

Garson still didn't have a single close friend. No one like Toby Hanson. Toby and he were best buds in North Carolina. Both of their dads were Marine officers stationed at Camp LeJeune. But since Garson and his mother moved away, he had only seen Toby once, when he and his mom returned to Lejeune for a visit. That was three years ago. At first, they had talked pretty often on the phone, almost every week. But as time went by, not so much.

Here in Pinewood, Garson felt like he didn't fit in. And he struggled with a gnawing anger because his dad wasn't here. That would've made everything better. Especially when kids hassled him or asked hurtful questions. "Why did your dad have to go away? Why didn't he stay with you and your mom?" And worst, "Isn't he coming back?"

It was tough for Garson to hear, much less respond. No matter what his mom told him, no matter how optimistic she tried to be, that last question continued to haunt him. It had been so long.

The worst of the kids was Billy Cribbs. Look in the dictionary under "bully" and there, Garson thought, should be a picture of Billy's sneering mug. And his coconspirator, Todd Ulander, was always with him. The biggest kid in fifth grade, he acted like Billy's bodyguard.

"Hey Stra-a-a-nge," Billy would howl, "Where you shufflin' off to?"

And that toad, Todd Ulander, would chime in "Yeah, Stra-a-a-nge" followed by his sniggering donkey laugh. What Garson hated most was how other kids then stared at him. What did they expect? Like he was going to punch out his tormentors?

Creeps, both of them!

Chapter 10
The Map

They finished lunch. Mrs. Strangewalker gathered the plastic bags, napkins and soda cans into her shopping bag. "Don't be too long. I'll be home in a couple of hours. I'm planning burgers on the grill with the potato salad I made yesterday."

"See ya then," Garson muttered after his mom kissed his cheek, which he usually didn't mind. In front of Mr. Rock, it embarrassed him. He wanted to appear more than a little kid to his soon-to-be science teacher.

Content that Garson was in good company, she shook Mr. Rock's hand and left. Then scientist and apprentice got down to business.

Mr. Rock unfolded a map, the very one he used and annotated when he studied the Shining Mountain Glacier forty years ago. He spread it on the picnic table. As if a treasure map, the features and hand-written notes riveted Garson.

The science teacher explained some of his research along the glacier's northern edge. "My work was at one point in time. Those measurements need repeating to record any changes."

Garson nodded eagerly in agreement. "Like they've been doing in Glacier Park."

"Exactly. Most results of climate change are gradual; not sudden or obvious, like a hurricane or a forest fire. Although such natural events are increasing in frequency and intensity, some people don't see the connection to the global climate. Or they simply choose to ignore it."

Garson was shaking his head. "But how can they ignore it's happening?"

"Sometimes people need to see things for themselves. It needs to feel *real.* That's part of the job of science. It's why I wanted to study glaciers, way back when climate change was an emerging concern. Melting glaciers are undeniable proof of the warming climate. Like an ice cube that melts when removed from the freezer."

Garson learned a lot about the science of climate change in his reading about glaciers. Today he wasn't reading about the scientists who did the studies. He was actually talking to one!

He peered at the map. "Like you said, someone needs to go back up there and do what you did."

Mr. Rock looked intently at Garson. This was not a task for the faint of heart. When he was sure he had the boy's full attention he said, "Getting there isn't easy. There's a trail to this lake," his finger pointing to a blue splotch on the map. "After the lake, it's a bushwhack through the forest. It's steep. When I used to hike there, I followed whatever route I could find. But it was tough going. Thank goodness for the deer and elk. I followed their trails, so I didn't have to bust through brush up 2,000 feet of ugly!"

Garson's eyes were big as golf balls, listening to the geologist's stories of clambering up the mountain and sudden snow squalls he braved to study the glacier. Among the map's captivating details, he focused on the penciled route Mr. Rock had sketched from Lupine Lake's western shore, through the forest, to the alpine zone above. The glacier was way up there.

"I'd like to do it."

Mr. Rock's eyes twinkled, "I thought so."

He brushed the hair back from his forehead and began explaining the more straightforward parts of his work. The parts a twelve-year-old boy might repeat.

"This would make quite a project for next school year's science fair."

Garson beamed.

"But like I said, getting there will be the hardest part. Maybe your dad could go with you?"

"I don't think so."

"Oh? Why not?"

"He's not here."

"No hurry. You won't be going up there until September."

"Not until September?"

"Do you know how to conduct a scientific study?"

Garson scrunched his forehead, "I'm not sure."

"That's what sixth-grade science class is about. The scientific method. You'll need to learn how scientists do their work so your project is science, not just a long hike to take some measurements," Mr. Rock paused, wondering if he was being harsh. He didn't want to curb the boy's enthusiasm.

"It's like deciding to play a sport you've never played before and thinking you know how to do it because you read about it or watched someone else. We don't really know what science is until we do it. Science is a process, a set of steps. First, you must learn the process, the scientific method. You'll see in September, in the first weeks of class. Then your dad can go with you to the glacier."

"Doesn't matter. He won't be here then." Almost in a whisper, he added, "He's in Afghanistan. I don't know when he's coming back."

The change in Garson's expression was instantaneous. His face tensed. His eyes were downcast. He began to fidget.

Reflexively he ran his thumb over the jackknife's inlaid message, "Garson from dad."

Mr. Rock was certain there was more to the story. A soldier's son was sure to know when his father's deployment was scheduled to end, when he'd be returning home.

Seeing Garson's unease, he said, "Maybe someone else can go with you. Either way, you'll need to learn some outdoor skills. Do you know how to use a map and compass?

Garson shook his head no.

"Lesson one in mountaineering."

He showed Garson how to use a topographic map and compass to "orienteer."

"This is how you read the details on the map." He guided Garson's eyes from the map's squiggly lines and symbols to the legend, explaining each of the symbols.

"This is how to use the compass to orient the map toward true north. And then to determine how to get to a destination."

Next, he pulled out his old altimeter.

"With a USGS map, a compass, and this nifty device, you can find your location anywhere in the mountains. Maybe not quite as accurately as a GPS unit can, but for decades, before GPS was available to civilians, this is how we did it. It still works and requires no batteries," he chuckled.

He had Garson practice doing some simple orienteering. He showed him how to read and adjust the altimeter.

"Passing grade," the teacher announced with a broad smile.

"So, I can do it?"

"There's still more to this."

"Like what?"

"I need to teach you exactly how to repeat what I did at the glacier. You need to practice. And ... I need to be convinced you can do it. But first, let's make sure your mom is okay with you doing the project. If she is, we could do lesson number two next Saturday."

Garson was ecstatic. Once school began this fall, he'd not only be in Mr. Rock's science class, but he'd be doing a science project on the Shining Mountain Glacier.

The next two Saturdays he rode his bike to the soccer field. No ferry by Subaru. His mom had reached a new level of cool in his opinion.

Garson was an eager student and Mr. Rock was impressed with his enthusiasm. Like a sponge absorbing water, Garson followed as Mr. Rock pointed out the numbered "Xs" on his map marking the reference points, how to make the measurements, and how to take repeat photographs of the ones Mr. Rock took forty years earlier.

"Before you go to the glacier, I'll provide everything you need: the map, compass, altimeter, and a couple of rolls of film."

Mr. Rock thought it best to retake the photographs with the same camera and type of film he had used originally. He still had his old Nikkormat 35mm SLR. He enjoyed photographing nature with it and kept a supply of film in his freezer.

He demonstrated, then made Garson repeat, how to load film and use the controls to take properly exposed images. "Practice makes perfect," he liked to say.

Finally, he showed him how to use a compact GPS. With it, Garson could log waypoints for the reference points Mr. Rock had established along the margin of the glacier.

Garson was psyched!

After those final lessons on the Saturday before the school year began, Mr. Rock was convinced. Garson could do this. And for the first time in a long time, Garson was sure of something. He was sure he could do it too.

The sudden sight of the yellow Subaru jogged her. Mrs. Strangewalker was surprised she'd walked all the way back to the trailhead absorbed by the events leading up to this day. Her reflections so occupied her that she hadn't felt alone. Now she did. An image of Garson somewhere up on the mountain, alone, sent a shiver through her.

Eleven-thirty, the clock in the Subaru read. Garson said he'd be back by five. She winced. *I hope this book I brought is good. I'll need it to keep my mind occupied.*

Page after page, she tried to focus on the novel's story. Again and again, she had to reread a paragraph or more, as her mind wandered. *Should I have let him go on alone? Oh, please, I hope he's started down by now?*

At three o'clock, her cell phone rang.

"Hello," she answered anxiously.

"Mrs. Strangewalker?"

She recognized his baritone voice, "Yes, Mr. Rock. This is Lucy."

"I thought I'd call and see if you and Garson were doing okay."

Mr. Rock had insisted that Garson not hike to the glacier alone. The day before the hike, Lucy called to tell him she was going with Garson. She detected Mr. Rock's sigh of relief. He wished them luck and before their call ended, she gave him her cell phone number.

"Garson went on alone," she said, explaining how the hike was more than she could handle. "He's going to meet me back here at the trailhead by five o'clock."

The silence on the phone unsettled her. *He thinks I was wrong to let him go on alone,* she was certain.

"Sounds good. You're sure you're okay?"

"Yes."

"Well, it's good weather. Garson will be fine," he said to reassure himself as much as her. "You have my number. Please give me a call when he gets down. I want to be the second person to congratulate him."

Chapter 11

The Glacier

Upon leaving the forest, Garson stopped in his tracks ... Shining Mountain's sparkling summit pierced the sky. His skin tingled. *This ain't no picture in a book. It's a real glacier!*

Heat waves shimmered across its surface like he'd seen over the Atlantic Ocean's waters on a blistering summer's day. The snow's radiance made him squint.

With his goal now in view, his pace quickened. He scrambled across the alpine meadow, noting the faded flowers and intricate patterns of lichens encrusted on rock. He hopped over sparkling rivulets tumbling from the melting snow and ice above. A small flock of birds bolted from the ground. Noting their size and markings, he checked his field guide. *Rosy finches,* one of the alpine zone's few bird inhabitants.

What Garson didn't see, between the alpine tundra and the glacier, was something that identifies mountain icefields as glaciers. A moraine. Terminal moraines mark the farthest advance of mountain glaciers where the ice plowed up a wall of rocks during the Great Ice Age over 12,000 years ago. That a moraine was missing didn't dawn on Garson. That would only become clear in time, and quite wondrously. He was focused now on the glacier. *Look at all that ice.*

Trudging upward, ever closer to the ice, his lungs felt the alpine air grow thinner. His chest heaved. He focused on maintaining his pace.

As he hiked, Garson mentally rehearsed how he'd take the measurements and photographs—like a real scientist—when he reached the north side of the glacier. He angled to his right in that direction.

It was twelve-thirty when he arrived.

"Pretty good," he congratulated himself with a fist pump.

Slack-jawed, he stared at the gleaming expanse of white towering toward the mountain's summit. *I wonder if I'm even seeing the top?*

Air spilling off the ice was cool like the rush from an opened freezer door. Evaporating sweat cooled Garson's face and neck. He wanted to enjoy this euphoric experience to the fullest—his first time at a real glacier. *I've gotta stop and look at this for a while.*

On a block of rock, he sat facing the glacier. He pulled on a purple rain jacket retrieved from his pack. With his eyes barely leaving the glacier's terminal wall of ice, he ate his mom's sandwich and finished his water. A crystalline stream rushed by his feet before gurgling beneath the rocks. *No problem getting water here*, he smiled.

After the break, Garson strode deliberately around the mountain onto its north slope. The glacier's ominous rampart of ice chilled his left shoulder as he followed below its lower edge. Gradually, he angled lower as the ice descended in elevation. Here on the mountain's cooler, north side, the ice wasn't retreating as fast as it was on the less-shaded sides.

He'd learned from books and websites that glaciers waged a never-ending battle between the seasons. Winter and spring replenished them with snow; summer and early fall melted it away.

He'd read how summer and fall were winning the war with

the planet's glaciers. The ancient ice was in retreat. And he knew why. As more fossil fuels were burned, a thickening blanket of greenhouse gases warmed Earth's land and oceans. Bad news for glaciers everywhere.

If people understood what was happening, they might change what they were doing. With guidance and encouragement from Mr. Rock, maybe, just maybe, what he learned on Shining Mountain could help. Garson was stoked to try.

He stopped to check his position on the map. *I gotta be getting close to the first reference point.* There were ten evenly spaced reference points along the glacier's edge where Mr. Rock had taken his original photos. But when Garson checked the altimeter, something seemed wrong. According to the instrument's elevation reading, he should have been standing where the map showed the glacier! *What's wrong? I don't get it!*

Before leaving the trailhead, he'd adjusted the altimeter to match the elevation shown on the USGS map.

"Accurate elevation readings," Mr. Rock explained, "depend on constant barometric pressure, which changes as both the weather and elevation change. The altimeter senses barometric pressure which decreases at a predictable rate with increasing elevation."

Who knew?

"It's what makes the needle move as you go up or down a mountain," he said.

As Garson understood it, he must reset the elevation reading on the altimeter whenever he found himself at a spot of known elevation shown on a USGS map. Adjusting the reading was most important if the barometric pressure was changing, like if a weather system was blowing in.

No big change was predicted on the weather forecast last

evening. Since leaving the trailhead, the altimeter's reading should have changed only as a result of increasing altitude. The elevation reading here at the glacier's edge should be right. *Why wouldn't it be right?*

He tapped the altimeter's glass face. The needle jerked slightly and settled on the same reading—7,740 feet above sea level. That elevation on the map would have put Garson on top of dozens of feet of glacial ice. Something's not right. *What'd I do wrong?*

He pulled the GPS unit from his pack. With his teacher's help, Garson had logged into the GPS unit the approximate coordinates of Mr. Rock's ten reference points. Following the unit's directions to the most easterly reference point—#1 on the map—Garson found himself standing nearly a football field away from the glacier.

"I don't get it!" he said out loud.

Totally frustrated, he began searching for the reference point's marker. If the chunk of half-inch diameter rebar was still anchored in the ground, it would help solve this mystery. He walked in expanding concentric circles. His eyes scanned left and right as he hopped across the rocks, looking for a rusty steel stake poking two or three feet up.

"Hey! There it is," he shouted.

After four decades, it remained upright, wedged between the rocks. It was as steadfast as the nearby jagged boulder in the picture Mr. Rock took forty years ago. Even the steel tag remained fastened with heavy wire to the rebar.

"Wow!" he grinned. He could still read the embossed coding on the tag: RP #1 8-29-1979.

He visualized Mr. Rock bending over, pounding the stake there four decades earlier. "This is so cool!"

He tugged the altimeter from his pullover pocket. Staring

at the dial, he blinked, *Oh, I know what's happening.* The altimeter was correct. The reference point was right where it should be—right on the 7,600-foot contour line. The glacier was wrong!

The ice had receded from where it had been forty years ago, and from where it appeared on the USGS map. He looked for a date in the map's legend. "Whoa! 1966."

He felt his heart thumping. He couldn't remember the last time he felt so excited. *This is really going to work, at least for this first one.*

He debated whether to find the remaining reference points or start his work at this one. He looked at his watch—ten minutes after one o'clock. He pulled the second roll of surveyor's tape from his pack, snapped a piece from the roll, and tied it to the rebar. *I'll find all the stakes first. That should make it go faster.*

One by one, he found and flagged each stake. Some took longer to spot than others. Only one wasn't anchored in the ground, either bolt upright or cocked at an angle. With some searching, he found number seven. Where it lay between two rocks, it was in line with numbers six and eight, right on the 7,600-foot contour line. Wielding a rock as a hammer, he drove it into the ground.

Amazingly, tags were still attached to all ten stakes. *I'll be able to repeat what Mr. Rock did.*

Beginning at stake number ten, and working backward, he repeated the steps, just as Mr. Rock had instructed Garson to do. "Everything must be repeated exactly, for scientific consistency," Garson remembered him saying.

1. Attach the camera to the tripod, four- and one-half feet above the ground.
2. Aim and zoom the lens to duplicate the scene in Mr. Rock's photo, making sure it included any distinctive rocks in the

original photo.

3. Using the camera's manual settings, set the shutter speed and F-stop to obtain the maximum depth of field.
4. Focus the lens and take three photos: one slightly underexposed, one slightly overexposed, and one on the money.
5. Record the number of each photo and the GPS waypoint in his spiral notebook.

Those steps completed the repeat photography at each reference point. Three photos each at ten reference stakes. Two others taken back at the treeline. He still had four shots left on the thirty-six-exposure roll of film. At the final reference stake, Garson shot three more photos of the glacier with the lens zoomed out to wide-angle. He wanted these to remember how immense and incredible the glacier was, even though he couldn't fit it all in the photo.

After taking the photos at each reference point came the really exciting part. When Mr. Rock had studied the glacier, he had measured the distance from each of the reference stakes up the slope to the edge of the glacier. He recorded the compass bearing from the stake to the glacier to prevent errors when he remeasured in the future.

This took Garson far less time than it had taken Mr. Rock. His teacher had stretched a 100-foot tape from the rebar to the edge of the ice. Garson had a laser rangefinder. He simply stood at the stake, noted a target on the ice along the compass bearing, sighted the range finder on the target, and shazam! The rangefinder gave him a distance readout. Despite each reference point being farther from the glacier now, measuring and recording the distance only took a minute.

Garson didn't have Mr. Rock's original measurements with him. He could hardly wait to compare those with his. From the forty-year-old photos, he could see that the glacier had retreated. A lot!

Performing all these steps correctly might sound complicated. But Mr. Rock had trained Garson well.

Now I get it, Garson realized. *It's part of the scientific method he talked about in class.*

As a result of his practice at the soccer field, completing the steps at the glacier came naturally. It saved him time—something he didn't have enough of to waste.

After completing the photos and measurements, Garson suddenly felt tired. Very tired. He'd worked nonstop. Hadn't paused to eat his remaining food. Plopping onto a flat rock next to a gurgling rivulet, he ate the other half of his sandwich, some dried apple slices, and a granola bar. A long drink from the water bottle washed it down. He topped off the bottle and squeezed it beside the rangefinder in his pack.

Out of nowhere, a bird splashed through the water only yards from Garson. It wagged its tail back and forth, like a finger wagging, "No, no, no." From his field guide, he identified it as an American pipit.

"Pip-pit pip-pit," it called when it flew to the glacier. *Time I got going too,* Garson thought.

For the first time since he began the measurements, he looked at his watch. *Three forty-five! How can it be so late? There's no way I can get back by five o'clock.* A bolt of panic shot through him. *Mom's gonna really be worried, or worse. And I forgot to call her!*

Guilt prickled the back of his neck. He retrieved the phone from his pack and punched in her number. It rang twice, then disconnected. He stood up and tried again. One ring. Same result. "Stupid phone!"

He tucked the phone into his pack.

Rather than walking fast, he hopped from one chunk of

rock to the next. As he bounded down the alpine meadow, it happened. He miscalculated. The toe of his boot caught the edge of a rock. He tried to catch his balance but couldn't. As he hit the ground, pain stung his right leg.

"Owwwww!"

The pain was so sharp, it made him dizzy. He thought he'd throw up, or maybe pass out first. Drawing himself to a sitting position, he hunched over, shut his eyes, and tried to pull the right knee to his chest. But he couldn't. He opened his eyes. His hand was blood-stained from clutching his throbbing shin. Worse yet, he realized that his boot was wedged beneath a rock. He tugged but couldn't budge his right foot.

"Damn it!" he shouted.

He squatted onto his other leg to straighten the trapped one. Oh, that hurt. And no twisting and tugging would free his right foot.

His next thought was about the camera. Was it okay? Didn't want to damage that!

He slipped off the daypack and checked inside. Luckily, he thought, he'd fallen face first. The pack hadn't hit the ground. Instead, it slammed into the back of his head. He rubbed and felt a knot. The camera was fine, making the scrapes on his palms and aching leg feel not quite so bad.

Somehow, he had to free his imprisoned foot. He leaned his chest against the injured leg, hoping his boot might break loose as his ankle flexed. No luck. Instead, he thought it might get stuck worse. With his hands, he pushed the rock trapping his foot. It was too big. He couldn't budge it.

"Damn it!" he shouted again. *How am I going to get unstuck?*

A jolt of terror shot through him. He had to get back to the car. His mother was waiting. In a few hours, it would be dark. Then what?

His hand found the knife in his pocket. He gripped it as if his life depended on it. As his heart began to slow, a new dread crept over him. He was being watched.

Chapter 12
The Encounter

Getting back to Oreo consumed Buddy. Whenever the two were apart this long, she missed her so. And she had such news to tell her about the wolverine, and how Tenanmouw showed her the cliffs where the Shining Mountain band spent winter.

Ambling across the meadow, randomly nipping juicy grasses and sedges beside the glacier's meltwaters, she replayed her conversations with Tenanmouw. Like the last time, three weeks ago, she relished time with him. She learned so much. And of course, he'd now saved her life, twice.

"Whooosh!" A bird flushed at her feet, sending Buddy hopping sideways. Perfectly disguised in a plumage of mottled brown, it went winging and clucking upslope. In more than two months on Goat Mountain, she'd never seen a white-tailed ptarmigan. *What else might I have missed while I've been walking?* Her head swiveled from side to side, but there was nothing else to see across the meadow.

Now it was decision time. Travel south around the glacier or north, the way she had come. She guessed the time to trek back to Oreo would be about the same. She stopped to think it over, taking a long drink of water that danced and gurgled over glistening rocks.

I better go to the north. Tenanmouw said there won't be another wolverine there. I can't be sure if I go south.

By now the sun was past its midday zenith and arcing west. She picked up her pace. The faster she traveled, the less time some hungry beast would have to find her. Both Oreo and Tenanmouw had warned her that a small goat traveling alone invited trouble. She now knew they were right.

Up the mountain, she angled toward the glacier. She loved this cool place abounding with water and tasty plants. But she didn't dawdle. She cruised across the mountain's northern slope, following her shadow in the afternoon sun.

Where the land fell away to the east, more big rocks and boulders studded the alpine meadow. Rounding a boulder twice her height, she heard a cry.

"Owwwww!"

Buddy froze in her tracks. *What was that?*

The red-tailed hawk who soared beyond the ledge where she was born sometimes screamed. But not like this. She'd heard coyotes yip-howl, but this was no coyote. This sound she'd *never* heard before.

Down the ridge, she spotted something. Not a wolverine but something vaguely familiar. The sight rattled her. Her memory flashed back to the second day of her journey to Shining Mountain. It was the day after the bear attacked Oreo, when they became separated.

She'd been alone. Alone except for Whodare, the pygmy owl who'd befriended and then guided her around that awful place stripped of trees. The place Whodare called the wasteland. She'd been terrified there by a man who chased her. The shouts from wasteland man, however, were different from the piercing cry she'd heard ... the one from the man before her now.

Although he was still a ways away, Buddy thought this man was smaller than the wasteland man. Otherwise, he looked the same. A ripple of fear shook her, as it had before Whodare had decoyed wasteland man away from her. The owl saved Buddy from some awful harm, or worse. Buddy was sure of it.

Locked in her tracks beside the boulder, Buddy trembled. The man was hunched on the ground.

"Damn it," he shouted.

Besides other mountain goats, Buddy could talk with other kinds of animals. Maurice the marmot. He was the first. Roark the raven? Of course. Whodare the pygmy owl? Check. And others too, when conditions were right. It was her special talent.

But ... she didn't expect to understand a man. She never again wanted to even see one. Not after wasteland man had scared her as much as that bear Ursidarr had. She certainly wanted no part of talking to one. Besides, the sounds this one made, "Owwwww," and "Damn it," made no sense to her.

What to do? *He's between me and where I need to go. To get back to Oreo. There aren't enough boulders in the meadow. No way I can stay hidden.*

After the small man took the black thing off his back, he hardly moved, except for one leg. His back was toward Buddy. She watched. And she watched. Hoping the man would go away.

When he didn't, she cautiously edged toward him, zigzagging from one large rock to the next. Her heart beat faster as she crept closer. When a few feet away, she stopped.

From so close, his man scent was unmistakable. Although smaller than wasteland man, he was twice as big as her. She heard him mumbling as he pulled at one of his legs. She sensed there was something wrong with him. Yes, she could smell it. The same thing she smelled from Oreo's wounded shoulder. The smell of blood! It made her shudder.

For a long moment, she remained frozen, wondering what to do next. Suddenly, the small man twisted his head around and spotted Buddy. He stared wide-eyed at her; but he didn't do anything.

Buddy spoke, "Are you hurt?"

The small man's hand fidgeted in the pocket of his cargo pants. His eyes grew larger.

Garson wasn't afraid, more like dumbfounded. This animal was only feet away. More incredibly, he understood what it said!

Never before had he seen an animal like this. While researching glaciers, he'd seen pictures of different animals on websites. But few hoofed animals lived high in the mountains, and only two he recalled were all white. The Dall sheep lived in Alaska and northern Canada. That left only ... *This has gotta be a mountain goat!* All fluffy white, it looked, well, amazing. And it was standing *right there.*

Like hoary marmots and wolverines, he read that mountain goats lived among North America's highest peaks. They were at home where glaciers and permanent snow were found.

Because Mr. Rock hadn't mentioned goats on Shining Mountain, Garson didn't expect to see any. Now he was face to face with one. It's fleecy white coat, black eyes and nose resembled the Samoyed dog who lived at a house not far from his. However, this goat's rounder head was topped by a pair of short black horns.

It's beautiful! But did I imagine it talking to me? Impossible!

As they stared at each other, Buddy wondered if this had been a mistake. Perhaps she should run down the meadow, back to Oreo. Then she heard him speak.

"Did you ask if I was hurt?"

"Yes. You're bleeding."

"I don't understand. How can you talk to me? Aren't you a mountain goat?"

Buddy realized what was happening. She could communicate with the small man for the same reason she could talk to other animals during her journey to Shining Mountain. Need. When she or another needed help, she could do it. This special gift was one of the reasons Roark had chosen her to be the next goat-Keeper of the Legend of Shining Mountain.

Often, she had questioned why she lived when her mother had not. *Is there a reason why? Something I'm supposed to do?*

When she asked, Oreo simply told her, "Your purpose is to find how to contribute to the band."

Oreo's counsel, and Roark telling her about the Legend of Shining Mountain, compelled her to seek a new home for the Goat Mountain band. But might there be something more she was meant to do? Was this chance encounter part of it?

"I didn't know I could talk to a man. Not until now."

Garson felt his body relax, a little. "I'm not really a man. I'm still a boy, a kid."

"Me too. I'm a kid until I get older." Buddy looked at the boy's bloodstained pants, "Are you okay?"

"I think so. Except I can't stand up."

He pulled up his pant leg and frowned as he looked at the gash. "I need to stand up and see if my leg's alright."

From his squatting position, he grabbed his right ankle with both hands. Gingerly, he pulled. Buddy saw him grimace.

"I'm stuck. My foot's caught under this rock."

Buddy found this puzzling. She'd encountered two men in her short life. One had chased after a bird he could never catch. Now this one had his foot stuck in the rocks. *That's probably why I haven't seen more of them.*

"Maybe I can help," she offered, without giving the impulse much thought.

Garson was stunned. *Is this really happening? I'm actually talking with an animal, a mountain goat? And now it offers to help me?*

"How?" he said hesitantly.

Buddy furrowed her brow and pawed the ground with a front foot. Garson recoiled. She moved closer to the boy, closer than felt comfortable—to either of them. Her eyes remained locked on Garson. No telling what even a small man might do.

With some difficulty, Garson had managed to sit down. He had to. His left leg, the one he was squatting on, had gone numb. Still, the pain across the top of his right foot told him he couldn't stay sitting for long.

When Buddy stepped beside his foot, Garson asked nervously, "What are you doing?"

"When I push the rock you're stuck under, you push with your other foot," Buddy responded coolly. "If we can move it, you can pull your foot out."

Amazing, Garson thought. *This mountain goat's really smart.*

Buddy anchored her forehead against the coarse granite, making sure to avoid grinding her little horns into the angular, gray block. She sure didn't want to break those.

The rock was big. Still, she thought the two of them could move it, perhaps enough.

"Ready? Push," Buddy groaned, planting her hooves, stiffening her back, and driving her round little head into the rock.

"I'm pushing," Garson said, his face tightening into a scowl.

Through the covering of wavy hair, Buddy felt the rock bite the soft skin of her forehead. Still, she pushed harder. Every muscle in her thirty-pound body tensed and strained.

"I felt it move," Garson groaned. "Keep pushing."

Garson's pushing leg was shuddering. His face turned to a mask of red. Sweat soaked his forehead.

Buddy felt like her skull would burst.

With a decisive burst of effort, the boulder rocked backward, just enough. Garson's trapped foot shot from its prison, sending him sprawling onto his back. Luckily, the backpack kept him from whacking his head.

Buddy's head popped up from the granite. Garson's eyes were nearly as wide as the grin on his face.

"We did it," he shouted.

"Yahoo!" Buddy returned.

She had a strange and unexpected urge to nuzzle the boy. Garson fought back an overwhelming impulse to throw his arms around the goat. Both felt excited, but uncertain what to do next.

Instead of stomping a foot to express her unease, Buddy turned to directly face the boy, "My name is Buddy."

"My name's Garson. Thanks. You helped me get out."

"You're still bleeding. I can smell it."

Garson pulled up his pant leg. By now blood had run down his shin to his sock. He braced himself with his hands and stood, careful to favor his good leg. He hobbled a few steps and sat back down, "Yeah, it's okay. Just kinda sore."

"Maybe I ..."

Buddy's words were drowned by the whooshing and flapping of setting wings.

Chapter 13

A Meeting of Three

Only feet from Buddy, a raven plopped onto a rock. Across its coal-black feathers, a shaft of sunlight imparted a shimmering violet sheen. Wildly croaking and snapping its wicked-looking three-inch beak, the awesome bird startled Garson. He scooted his butt backward as if fleeing a ghost.

Never had Buddy seen Roark so ruffled.

"What are you doing?" Roark demanded.

Buddy was used to the raven dropping in unannounced. That wasn't unexpected. What jolted her was Roark's tone of voice. It left her speechless.

"Consorting with a man? You should know better! Especially after the wasteland."

"Consorting? I don't know what you ..."

Roark interrupted, "Have you forgotten the man who chased you there?"

"Garson's not a man. He's a boy."

Garson's eyes darted back and forth as if tracking the ball in a tennis match. *This is unreal. First, a mountain goat shows up and starts talking to me. Then it helps me get my foot unstuck. Now the goat's being chewed out by a raven! Am I dreaming? Did I knock myself out when I fell?*

He flexed his foot. The shot of pain through his injured leg was real enough. *Not dreaming.*

"He could be dangerous, and in ways we cannot know," the raven scolded.

Buddy felt crushed. "He was stuck in the rocks. I only tried to help him."

Roark fluffed his feathers and croaked a single "Rur-ruk" in resignation.

"Maybe I over-reacted. But I'm here to tell you, men are to be avoided. They damage the forest. They don't respect the ways of nature."

"Maybe ... maybe so. But he seems to mean no harm."

"Then why is he here, on Shining Mountain?"

Good question, Buddy thought. *Good question indeed.*

Garson was bewildered by what he was seeing. Although he'd been able to talk to Buddy before, he understood none of their back-and-forth bleating and squawking.

Buddy turned to Garson, "This is my ... friend, Roark. He was wondering why you've come to Shining Mountain."

What? All of that to ask me this one question? Garson's mind shot into overdrive. *Why do they care? And how could they begin to understand my science project? They're just animals.*

Before he could answer, Roark directed Buddy, "Be sure to tell me exactly what he says. Every word. I don't trust any men, tall or small."

While looking from Buddy to Roark, Garson was uncertain if the raven could understand him too. Watching Buddy translate his words to Roark cleared that up.

Garson spoke slowly, as though speaking methodically was necessary for a mountain goat to have any chance of understanding, "Do you know that the world is getting warmer?"

Catching himself, he restated his question, "I mean Shining Mountain and the other mountains. Do you know they're getting warmer each year?"

He didn't expect a positive response and was surprised when Buddy replied, "Spirit, the matriarch of our band, worries about it. Summers are warmer and longer, she says, compared to before."

The goats know! Questions ricocheted through Garson's head, but he kept from blurting them out. Regaining his focus, he explained he went to school in a town, while pointing down the mountain. But schools and science classes, and all the other details leading to his climbing here today, were certainly unfathomable things to a mountain goat whose life was so different from his, Garson thought. He simply said, "The warming worries me too. To learn more about it, I came to the glacier."

He wished his camera were digital. *Then I could show her what I'm doing here.*

"We, I mean my teacher and me, think the Shining Mountain Glacier is shrinking. How much snow falls each winter can't replace how much melts in summer. Everything that depends on the glacier might change."

"Everything?"

"Yeah, like plants and animals ... even ones up here." Garson paused, *I've gotta stick to what I know is fact.* "Well, that's my guess. But scientists think it'll be bad for lots of animals if it keeps getting warmer."

"Sci-en-tists?"

"Yeah, others like me who study this stuff."

Buddy tried to digest what the boy told him, seeing how it fit with what Spirit said. But also trying to tie it together with the message of the Legend.

"Well, have you fallen asleep?" Roark blurted. "What did he say? What's he up to?"

"Sorry, Roark. I was trying to put everything together."

Buddy related what the boy said. She added, "Garson and someone he called his teacher believe the glacier is shrinking because it's getting warmer. He didn't call it the Great Warming, but I wonder if men know about the Legend too?"

"Nonsense. Only the Legend Keepers know. And certainly not men!"

Buddy was pondering this when Roark said, "Ask him if his teacher or other men are coming."

"Are others coming up here to the glacier? Other men, like your teacher?"

By now Garson guessed the raven, and maybe Buddy, felt threatened by humans. "No. I don't think others will come here. Especially my teacher, Mr. Rock. He has a bad leg."

"Bad like yours?"

"No, worse. He can't hike up here."

Relieved that Roark would find this good news, Buddy said, "He doesn't think others are coming here. Not even Rock."

"Rock?"

"That's his teacher, I guess like you've been a teacher to me." Roark cawed a note of approval, which Buddy followed with a laugh, "Rock and Roark, the teachers."

Roark looked unamused.

Then the strangest thing happened. Roark hopped next to Buddy—something he'd not done before—and said, "You've done well to learn these things from the small man. Now tell him this, so he understands why his presence distresses us."

After Roark finished, Buddy told Garson, "Up here where the mountains touch the sky is where our ancestors have always lived—goats, ravens, and other animals. We fear the changes we see. And Roark believes men may be the cause of them."

The words struck Garson like a two-by-four. He felt a jolt of guilt. *The raven's right. We are responsible.*

"I'm just a boy. But I do want to learn what's happening to your glacier, and your home on Shining Mountain."

"Oh, this is not my home," Buddy said.

"What? I thought you said the mountain was your home," Garson replied, perplexed by the goat's words.

"My home is over there," she said, twisting her head toward the south. "Goat Mountain is my band's home. I came here to see if this would be a better place for us."

Garson's eyes followed Buddy's gesture, but Shining Mountain blocked his view of everything to the south.

"Why? Why didn't you stay there?"

"Because things are changing at my home."

"How did you know to come here?"

Buddy ignored Roark's squawking, "What's he saying? What's he saying?"

"It's the place goats took refuge long ago to survive the Great Warming." Buddy abruptly stopped. *Am I telling him too much? Can I trust him?*

Great Warming? How could this little mountain goat know that these mountains experienced a warming climate long ago? Garson's head was swimming.

Despite Roark's agitation, Buddy decided to add one thing more, "You've been to the glacier. Did you see the rocks there?"

"The rocks? Everything up there is rocks."

"Did you really see the rocks? How they are different from this part of the mountain and down below?"

Garson furrowed his brow. He tried to picture what the rocks near the glacier looked like. *What's different about them?* He reflexively rubbed his injured leg.

"I guess not. Why's that important?"

"You need to see for yourself. I can't say any more," Buddy said, recalling how even Spirit rejected the Shining Mountain

Legend. *How could Garson possibly believe it. And what right do I have to share it with him?*

This was way too much for Garson to wrap his head around. Goats and ravens were animals, incapable of rational thinking about things humans understood. *How could a mountain goat think about its future?*

As Buddy relayed her conversation with the boy to Roark, Garson glanced at his watch—5:15. He gasped, "I'm so late! I've gotta go."

While sitting, his right leg had stiffened. When he leapt to his feet, it buckled beneath the pressure. A wave of nausea surged. He sat back down to shoulder his pack, rather than bending over to reach it.

He unzipped the main pouch to retrieve the water bottle. He took a drink. He pulled out a Ziploc bag containing the remaining dried apple slices. The goat and raven stared at him. *No, I'm not going to offer them something to eat. Dad always said it's not good to feed wild animals, except birds ... and not this kind of bird!*

When the raven hopped toward him, he stuffed the Ziploc in his pocket. Roark squawked.

Buddy shook her head. "Food on your mind again, Roark? Or should I say, still?"

A cream-colored butterfly floated by. Roark speared but missed. "Drat!"

A moment later, a second followed behind, angling closer to the raven. Fatal mistake.

The insect approached innocently. Garson saw Roark tilt his head to the side. He was obviously left eye dominant, the one he used for targeting prey at close range. Tilt head right; left eye aims; stab bug with big beak.

As his prey fluttered within range, Roark's head shot forward and the butterfly fluttered no more. In one smooth motion, he tipped his head and gulped it down.

"Wow," Garson said.

"I know. He's pretty good," Buddy quipped. "I've seen it plenty of times."

"And I thought ravens just ate roadkill."

"Roadkill? What's that?"

Of course, Garson realized, *how could this mountain goat know what roadkill is? You need roads for roadkill.*

"Roadkill is dead animals found where I live."

"What's he saying," Roark demanded.

Buddy translated and Roark responded with a loud, "Crääk."

Roark occasionally ventured below, down-mountain where the humans lived. A few times he'd dined on roadkill: deer, rabbit, raccoon, even skunk (ewe!). Yet above all else, he felt duty-bound as the raven-Keeper of the Legend, to remain in the mountains. It was his calling, his commission.

"What'd he say?" Garson asked in response to Roark's reaction.

"Oh, nothing important," Buddy said, fighting hard to suppress a belly laugh.

"I guess Roark likes bugs the way other ravens like roadkill."

"You have no idea," Buddy rolled her eyes.

Garson gazed at these two sentient creatures and thought how simple a raven or goat's life must be. Food, water, shelter when needed, and friends, as these two obviously were. Then it struck him. *What's happening to the glacier could be bad for them.*

Garson glanced at his watch again. *Oh, boy.* As he reshuffled the contents of his daypack, Buddy saw a strange look cross his face. A look of alarm.

Where is it? It's gotta be here. But indeed, the bird field guide was missing.

Failing to spot it on the ground nearby, he strained to remember when he saw it last. *I used it to identify the American pipit I saw at reference point #1. Right before I started down the mountain.*

"I can't believe I left it," he muttered.

His first instinct was to run to the glacier to get it. But he was already going to be really late. *What if mom calls out a search party? I'll never hear the end of that at school from Billy Cribbs and Todd Ulander. Besides, going back up there won't be good for my leg. I'll ... I'll have to come back.*

There's no way he'd leave the field guide on the mountain. Luckily, it was in a Ziploc bag should it rain, or worse yet, snow.

"I have to come back here. I left something at the glacier," he said, hoisting the pack onto his back.

"What's he saying? What's the matter?" Roark could tell by the boy's expression something was wrong.

"What?" Buddy asked Garson, ignoring Roark's questions.

"Something important. My dad gave it to me. I'd get it now, but my mom is waiting for me down there," he pointed.

"What?" Roark croaked louder.

Buddy summarized.

Instantly, Roark went off on his distrust of humans. "You've seen the wasteland. That's a taste of what they do. And now he's coming back?" Roark rasped his disapproval as he hopped from foot to foot.

"Is he alright?" Garson asked, wondering what the raven might do next.

"It's just ... well, I don't think he trusts men."

"Not all men are alike," Garson replied. "Are all goats the same?"

As each of the band members flashed through her mind, Buddy recalled how they were each very different. Ignoring

Garson's question, she said, "Don't worry. Roark will be alright."

"If I come back next weekend, will you show me the rocks? The ones at the glacier? And tell me why they're important?"

"First, Roark and I need to know something. Especially Roark." Buddy's eyes fixed on Garson. "Is what you came here to do at Shining Mountain going to help?"

For the first time, he detected dread in Buddy's voice. Garson knew his simple project was only that, a school science fair project. Nothing more. *But maybe, maybe I can make it something more. Something that really makes a difference.*

"I don't know for sure, but I hope so." Garson examined his surroundings, "Shining Mountain, the glacier and everything up here ... it needs to be protected."

Feeling more positive about how he'd react, Buddy summarized Garson's words for his squawking friend.

Not waiting for a contemplative pause by Roark to pass, she said to Garson, "Second thing. What's a weekend?"

"Oh, I mean seven days from now?"

"Seven days?" Buddy was confused. "You mean seven sleeps?"

I get it, Garson realized. *Goats count the days by nights.* "Yeah, seven sleeps. "Can I meet you right here?"

Buddy agreed. The plan was set.

Before leaving, Garson spied something higher up the mountain. A boulder splotched with a striking pattern of pale green and orange lichen. He retrieved the camera from his pack and photographed the boulder, so he wouldn't forget their meeting spot. The goat and raven exchanged quizzical looks. Roark croaked something Buddy was glad Garson couldn't understand.

Chapter 14
A Dubious Deal

As the boy grew smaller, striding toward the krumholtz and the forest beyond, Buddy asked Roark, "You're not angry with me anymore, are you?"

"I don't like it. Not one bit. The problem is, he's only one of so many down there," Roark trained his beak in Garson's direction. He stabbed the air as if spearing a moth. "I've seen them."

Buddy's forehead furrowed.

"It's best they are not among us. Men and animals should live apart," Roark scoffed.

"Why?"

"Because of what they do."

"You mean roadkill?"

"Roadkill, the wasteland, and far worse. Things you wouldn't understand or believe. As I said before, men don't respect the ways of nature."

They were silent for a bit. Buddy avoided Roark's stare, wishing an absent-minded bug would fly by. *Maybe he gets this way when he's hungry.*

"I don't know about men the way you do. I've only seen two. Garson isn't at all like wasteland man. Maybe it's because he's not grown to be a man yet. Maybe boys are friendlier and gentler."

In a timid voice, Buddy added, "I think he might help us."

"Help? What help do we need from a man, even a small man?" Roark's response was quick and harsh.

"Well, I can't stop thinking about one word he said? Did I tell you this? He said if the glacier keeps melting, everything that depends on the glacier might change."

Roark issued a curt "Cur-ruk."

"Everything. Plants, animals ... maybe us. The men he called scientists think so."

"Marmot manure."

Casting the remark aside with a toss of her head, Buddy persisted, "Maybe the changes Spirit and Tenanmouw talk about could be worse than they think or dare to say."

Roark was becoming more agitated, more than marmot manure upset. Indubitably, he was skeptical about trusting Garson, or any human. And teaming up with one? Well, he was as likely to hitch a ride on a lightning bolt.

Buddy wished she could talk once more to Mystic, the matriarch of the Shining Mountain band. Her words on the day when Buddy and Oreo arrived here were haunting. It was after Buddy told Mystic that she journeyed to Shining Mountain because conditions were getting worse for her band on Goat Mountain. "Our band is in trouble. I came here to see if this might be a better home."

In response, Mystic had said, "What affects one goat, or one band, affects us all."

Her words were unforgettable. *But what exactly did Mystic mean? Was she foretelling what's to come? I think so. I've gotta find a way to convince Roark that we should trust Garson.*

Roark cocked his head as another raven glided high above. He looked distracted but his mind was digesting what Buddy had said.

"Help from a man. Really?" he croaked dismissively.

"Do you remember what Battenmouw told you? The day he agreed to pass the mantle of goat-Keeper of the Legend on to me?"

"The old goat was unusually chatty that day. You can't expect me to remember *everything* he said."

"I remember it. Battenmouw said to you, 'I suppose at some time the goat-Keeper will need more than a fancy name. The Legend will need a goat-Keeper who has vision and courage. That kid goat, Buddy, has both. Seems she has a destiny to look after our band ... and maybe save it.'"

Buddy held her gaze on Roark. He scratched the top of his head with a toe. What had been a sunny day suddenly changed. From the northwest, a stiff wind sprang up. Graupel, round snow pellets, began pelting them.

What's this? Roark mused. *Now she can change the weather too, not just change my mind?*

"Well then answer me this with all your vision of the future. What does the future hold for us? And what value is a boy to goats and ravens? Indeed, one who gets stuck in rocks?"

Buddy didn't expect such a direct challenge. Doubt pierced her.

"I'm really not sure. I wish I were. But from all I've learned from Spirit, Mystic, and you, Roark, we can't wait until things get worse. Even if we don't know how much worse they might get."

"You and Oreo can bring your band here, as the leader of the Goat Mountain band did during the Great Warming."

"What if coming here isn't enough? What if things get worse here, too?" Buddy related Mystic's warning to her.

Roark saw where this was going. "Maybe there's nothing goats and ravens can do to change the future. And whatever makes you think that *boy* can?"

Buddy was thankful for a distraction interrupting Roark's stare. A small animal scurried from beneath a nearby rock. A vole. One Buddy guessed was born recently. It was gray with stubby face, short tail, and no bigger than a bottle cap.

Roark's left eye lasered on the would-be snack. The vole suspected nothing. With the speed of a stretched rubber band, the raven's foot sprang out and snatched the rodent. Roark cocked his head to swallow the bite-sized meal. The vole had other ideas. Before heading toward Roark's belly, it apparently nipped the raven's tongue. Roark let out a hideous squawk and spat the vole at his feet. Staggered and soggy with raven spit, it quivered and began hobbling away. Roark pinned it with a foot, swiftly lifted the victim to his beak, and down the hatch it went.

Buddy detected a faint squeak. It sent a shiver up her spine as she recalled TS, a relative of Roark's snack whom she had befriended.

"Where was I ..." Roark croaked and cleared his throat. "Oh yes, there's something else. How is it you could talk to Garson, and he to you? He's not an animal. He's a man."

"Not a man. A boy."

"Whatever. It's still very unusual."

"I was surprised too. But I think it's the same reason I can talk to other animals. Need. When I've needed help, from my marmot friend Maurice or Whodare the pygmy owl, I could talk to them. And then there's TS. From him I learned that when someone needs my help, I can talk to them too! It works both ways."

"TS? What's a TS?"

"Oh, of course. You don't know TS. He's the vole I met on my way to Shining Mountain. After the bear, Ursidarr, attacked Oreo and we were separated, I ..."

"You said a *vole*?" Roark interrupted.

"Yes, like the one you just ate. TS is short for Terror Stricken. I think you know why that name might suit a vole."

Roark stretched his neck forward and shook his head, "So, where is this vole."

"No way I'm telling you where TS lives," Buddy quipped. "Anyway, I could talk to Garson, I think, because he needed help. And maybe because we could use his help."

"Leave me out of this."

"Roark, the Legend's important. You know that too. You're the raven-Keeper who helped preserve it. I only know about the Legend because of you."

"Cur-ruk."

"Why did you and all the other raven- and goat-Keepers carry on the Legend for so long? It must be for our benefit."

Roark directed his gaze where the boy had vanished.

"Now we need to heed its message. I believe the Legend warns of the Great Warming's return." She paused for effect. "And I think you believe it too."

Buddy felt sure she was right.

"I think you won't say it because you don't know what to do about it," she said with such certainty it surprised her.

"I'll ask again," Roark challenged. "What could that boy Garson possibly do to make me want to trust him?"

"He said he came up here to learn if Shining Mountain's glacier is melting. And how fast."

"Don't see how that helps us. Do you?"

Buddy scrunched her forehead and stomped the ground with a front foot. "I don't know."

"Well, that's reassuring," Roark snapped.

"I know, let's ask him."

The boy was already planning to come back, in seven sleeps.

Roark couldn't prevent it. "So it shall be. You ask him."

Buddy felt relieved. Other than Oreo, Roark was most important in her life, and equally responsible *for* her life. He had led Oreo to her when she was three days old and on death's doorstep. Because they now shared the charge of the Legend Keepers, her unique bond with Roark would endure throughout their lives. If only Roark could be more trusting ... and learn some table manners!

Chapter 15

Secrets

Garson hobbled down the meadow, testing his leg. He soon got used to the pain, which wasn't as bad as he'd feared. His pace quickened.

Into a freshening wind, he looked behind him. They were still there. *I really did talk to a mountain goat. And it translated what I said to a raven!* He shook his head and grinned ear to ear. *No one would believe this. Not in a million years!*

As he muscled his way through the tangled and twisted branches of krumholtz, graupel pellets began hailing down. Small though they were, the frozen blobs stung his neck. For protection, he shoved his hands into his pockets. Ahhhh, the jackknife. *I think dad would be proud of me.*

When he spotted the first flutter of hot pink, he thought of Mr. Rock. Without these guideposts, he could've gotten lost in the forest for who knows how long.

At the first big whitebark pine, he sat and leaned his back against the trunk. First order of business: call again. *I'll try Mr. Rock this time.* Anxiously, he punched in the number from the paper in the phone case. After three rings, Mr. Rock picked up. Garson's heart thumped.

"Mr. Rock. It's me, Garson. I called but couldn't get my mom. Let her know, if you can, I'm heading down the mountain. Tell her I'm sorry I couldn't call her. Mr. Rock? Mr. Rock? Are you there?"

Silence. *Maybe he heard me.*

Next, his leg. With a cotton bandana, he dabbed water and scrubbed his leg and blood-soaked sock. The better he could make it look, the less alarmed his mom would be. He took a long drink of glacier-cold water, washing down the last dried apple slices. In less than five minutes, he was back on the trail.

Flag by flag he navigated through the forest. At a place he hadn't noticed on the trudge up the mountain, he stopped. A grove of quaking aspen trees commanded a tiny opening. Their ivory trunks and branches contrasted with the dreary conifer forest. Looking through a canopy of golden leaves, he realized the snow had stopped and the clouds were mostly gone.

One more thing he couldn't miss. In front of his boots was a huge pile of bear poop. Hand squeezing the cannister of pepper spray, his eyes darted left and right. Nothing. And not a sound except a Clark's nutcracker chattering in a treetop.

Garson checked his watch. *Oh, boy!* He didn't stop again. Not at the meadow at Lupine Lake, where he'd left his mom. Not at the driftwood log where they snacked. Not until he spotted the yellow Subaru.

At 6:00 pm, Mrs. Strangewalker's phone rang.

"Hello."

"Has Garson returned yet?" As he spoke, Mr. Rock realized his voice sounded more anxious than he wished. She had said she'd call him as soon as Garson returned to the trailhead. He was now an hour overdue.

"No. Not yet," her voice wavered.

She paused.

"Honestly, I'm beginning to worry. The sky's gotten dark and it's getting colder here."

"He called me a few minutes ago. The connection was bad. His words were garbled and then we got cut off. I called the number back but no luck."

"What did he say? Was he alright?"

Mr. Rock paused, "I heard him say he was heading down the mountain. The rest I couldn't understand. I'd like to drive up and wait there with you if that's alright."

"Yes. I could use the company."

He thought he heard relief in her voice.

Mr. Rock arrived before Garson reached the trailhead. She filled him in about hiking with Garson to the end of the lake.

"I tried hiking up the mountain with him. But my asthma ... I just couldn't do it," she felt tears welling in her eyes.

"I feel terrible for letting him go on his own. Do you think we should call the sheriff? To organize a search party?"

Tears spilled down her cheeks.

"Mom," Garson yelled, sounding as upbeat as possible. His watch read 6:45. He was almost two hours late.

"Garson," she dashed to meet him. "Are you alright?"

"Yeah. I'm fine. I'm really sorry I'm late." On the hike down, he'd pledged to be forthcoming as he could about the trip, including his leg. Still, he had plenty he didn't want to share. Who would believe him anyway?

She released him from her bear hug. Wiping the tears from her cheeks, she said, "Mr. Rock said you called him."

"I did, after I tried calling you and it wouldn't go through."

"That's alright. He came to meet you."

Garson had seen the gray pickup truck parked next to the Subaru. His teacher stood back while mom and son embraced. Then he hobbled forward, smiling broadly.

Near the trailhead, all three sat on the trunk of a fallen

tree. Garson between them with his mother's arm around his shoulders. He described his hike to the glacier—how he'd found all ten reference points and retaken the photographs and measurements, the way Mr. Rock had shown him. He knew he made it sound like finding the reference stakes was harder and took longer than it actually had.

"Yeah," he answered Mr. Rock, "the camera worked fine. But I guess we won't know until we get the pictures back."

"I knew you could do it," he beamed. "The pictures will turn out fine."

"Hanging those pink flags worked great. Not sure I would've made it down this easy if you hadn't told me to do that."

"Are you sure you're alright?" his mom pressed.

"Well, I banged my leg on a rock," he pulled his pant leg up and saw her wince. "It's really not so bad," he quickly said. He now wished he'd stuck band-aids across the jagged gash to hide it.

"Doesn't look too serious," Mr. Rock said, to ease the anguish in Mrs. Strangewalker's face.

"Let's get you home, so I can clean and put some antibiotic on that. And get some food in your stomach. It's after seven," she said with a glance at her watch. "You must be starved."

"Mr. Rock ..." she began.

"Please call me Doc. It's what my friends call me."

"Okay. Would you like to join us for dinner? It's the least I can do to repay you for your concern and for driving all the way up here."

"Thanks for the invitation, Lucy. The two of you must be exhausted and have lots to talk about. Maybe another time." He patted Garson's shoulder.

As the Subaru bumped and lurched toward Pinewood, a tug of war raged in Garson's head. *I gotta tell her about Buddy. No, I can't.*

Garson chatted on about the withering wildflowers, the views from the mountain, and especially the glacier. "It was so cool actually being there, seeing it up close ... not just in books or the internet."

He told her again about looking for the reference stakes and using the camera "to do what Mr. Rock did long ago." The words "long ago" struck her, a jolting reminder. So many years had slipped by since her husband John had been gone.

Continuing the chatter, Garson left little opening for her to ask questions. Questions he might not want to answer. Besides, his mom worried about him most when he was quiet. Was he struggling with any number of things: school, especially the boys who bullied him there, and mostly missing his father? As much as she tried, she couldn't be both parents to him. She struggled with that. Hearing Garson so enthusiastic about seeing the glacier cheered her.

At home, they ate leftovers. After showering, each collapsed in bed. During the night she checked his room upstairs, just to be certain he was really there.

The next week Garson spent in a fog. He attended classes on auto pilot, like watching someone else going through the motions. Garson, the real Garson, was preoccupied with what consumed him: glaciers, mountain goats, ravens, and how global warming might harm them.

Walking down the hall on Monday, he failed to spot Billy

Cribbs and Todd Ulander waiting for him to pass by. Suddenly he tripped and crashed headlong into a row of student lockers. The racket triggered a chorus of laughter from students.

"Well, aren't you the klutz," Billy barked. "Yeah, a real Straaaaange Walker," Todd chimed in with his disgusting donkey laugh.

Idiot! Garson said to himself. *I might as well have been staring at a three by five, letting Cribbs trip me like that.* He tried more than ever to avoid them the rest of the week.

The next day things got worse.

"I've got to be at work early tomorrow," his mom had said. "I'll have to leave before you go to school. Okay?"

"Sure."

"I'll put your lunch on the table. Oh, and be sure to lock the door when you leave, sweetheart."

Garson was still in his room when he heard her leave. He dressed, brushed his teeth, and returned to his computer. He checked the weekend weather forecast, then Googled "mountain goats." He began clicking weblinks.

He was about to begin a new search "mountain goats and climate change" when he noticed the time in the lower right corner of the screen. "Crap!" he hollered.

His first class was about to begin. Lunch in hand, he locked the front door behind him, and pedaled his bike lightning fast to school. When he opened the door to Mrs. Cullen's classroom, he felt fifteen pair of eyes harpoon him.

With downcast eyes, he walked past his teacher and quietly said, "Sorry I'm late."

English wasn't his favorite subject. Punctuation, sentence structure ... it didn't interest him. But he liked Mrs. Cullen. She seemed fair and really interested in students learning to understand what they read, and especially how to write well.

Her stinging look and the classroom murmurs were more excruciating than having a tooth pulled.

At the end of class, Mrs. Cullen said, "Garson, please remain here. I need to talk to you."

She marched him to the principal's office. Following an unpleasant grilling and warning about future tardiness, Garson said, "It won't happen again. But ... do you have to tell my mom?"

"That's for me to decide," Mr. Humphner said. "In the meantime, no more tardiness without an explanation in advance from home."

Garson's mother never found out. He guessed Mrs. Cullen went to bat for him, rocketing her near the top of his favorites list.

After finishing homework each evening, Garson checked Saturday's weather forecast. Was good weather going to hold? If a hint of snow was forecast, he could always return to the website later, hoping for a better prediction.

Then, he resumed researching mountain goats and ravens. Ravens, he learned, are highly vocal. One website explained how bird biologists had identified thirty-three different calls made by ravens. Each probably represented distinct words or phrases. *Wow! Ravens must be really smart. Maybe why they can talk to mountain goats.*

But nothing he read remotely suggested a mountain goat could talk to other animals. Certainly not to people!

His mother nearly had to drag him from his computer to get some sleep each night. But not when he went to bed, nor when he got up, would that voice leave his head.

You have to tell her.

Okay! Someday I'll tell her about Buddy. But not yet.

Of course, what he couldn't avoid telling her, or rather asking her, was to go back to Shining Mountain on Saturday. "After seven sleeps," he mouthed, picturing Buddy's woolly white image in his mind.

Sunday, Monday, Tuesday. Each day he vowed he'd tell his mom he needed to return for his book. *But how do I tell her so she won't say no?*

He'd talk to her ... because he must. If he didn't show on Saturday, he'd be letting Buddy down. And himself. "Did you see the rocks?" she had asked him. What did she mean? Why would she ask me that if it wasn't important? I've gotta find out.

Besides his promise to Buddy, Garson had to go for his dad. The Swiss Army knife and bird field guide his dad gave him were Garson's most prized possessions. Leaving the book to rot on the mountain would be abandoning a precious connection to him. The thought of it was agonizing.

By Wednesday, Garson was bursting at the seams to tell someone about Buddy and Roark. *How cool? I know their names!*

Most times it didn't bother him. Now he wished he had a friend to tell. Someone he could completely trust. Someone who would cross their heart and hope to die if they didn't keep his secret.

But Garson didn't have friends. Much less, one to confide in.

Then it struck him, *Toby. I could call Toby and tell him.*

He and Toby could talk about anything when they were both in North Carolina. They were six or seven then. Now they were twelve. But what difference should that make?

Besides, trusting Toby with his story about Buddy and Roark would be safer than telling someone in Pinewood. Here, it was sure to get out. Most important, *I can ask Toby how to convince my mom about Saturday*. There weren't many sleeps left until then.

He would call Toby that evening, he promised himself.

Chapter 16
Waiting

Wednesday, September 18

It was the end of classes on Wednesday. Instead of going straight home, Garson walked the hallway to Mr. Rock's classroom. Seventh grade science had ended. He waited outside as the students filtered out. One of the last was Kira, the girl with freckles and red hair who he met at the arts and science festival last spring. "Get ready. Here it goes," she had announced as her paper mache volcano erupted.

Because she was a year ahead of him, they shared no classes. Since school began, Garson had only seen her in the halls. She was wearing blue shorts and a white blouse today. Her hair was deeper red than he remembered and fell to her shoulders, not in tight curls, but more like flowing waves. She caught him looking her way and said, "Hi."

"Hi," Garson replied faintly.

He felt his pulse quicken as she stopped in front of him. "I heard you're doing a project on glaciers for the science fair."

Garson was stunned.

When no sounds came from his mouth, Kira continued, "Mr. Rock mentioned it in science class this week. In his lecture about climate change."

"He said I was doing it?"

"No. I figured that out on my own."

"How?" he would have squeezed the jackknife in a death grip about now.

"Well, he said someone in his sixth-grade class was doing it. I remembered you asking questions about glaciers at the arts and science festival last spring. Two plus two equals you."

Garson felt his face and neck getting warm. Like when Mrs. Cullen called on him with a question about verb conjugations and his mind went blank.

"Besides, it had to be somebody who could hike up there. Or want to."

This was getting super uncomfortable. Garson wasn't interested in girls, much less older ones. After momentarily feeling flattered that she stopped to talk to him, now he was overwhelmed by one thought, *How can I end this?*

"Well, was I right?" she tilted her head and raised her eyebrows.

"Uh, yeah. I am. I hiked to Shining Mountain Glacier last weekend."

"Cool! I might try out for the Science Olympiad team. The competition's coming up in November. At the university."

"Wow. That's great!" Garson wondered how the words had come out. Had he sounded sincere? Or dumb!

"And I'm gonna do a project for Science Fair too. Only I don't have a good idea yet," she frowned.

Garson felt a sense of normalcy returning, like he surfaced from holding his breath underwater for too long.

A voice from down the hall called, "Are you coming, Kira?"

"Oh, I've gotta go. Good luck with your glacier project."

Before he could reply she spun and was down the hall.

Garson wasn't sure, but he thought, just maybe, he had said goodbye to her.

"Garson, good to see you again."

Shaken from what seemed like a daydream, Kira had morphed into his science teacher.

"Hi Mr. Rock."

Mr. Rock taught both sixth and seventh grade science, plus geography. Seventh grade science was his last class of the day.

Over one shoulder was the same tan rucksack he had with him the first day they had met at the park this summer. Mr. Rock's toothy smile brought Garson back to their joint venture on the Shining Mountain Glacier.

"Film is in the mail. We might have the developed slides back next week."

He had told Garson that Ektachrome produced color slide images, not prints. Prints would then need to be made from the slides.

"Oh, next week."

"You were thinking sooner?"

Garson nodded.

"Time by mail to the lab and back takes at least a week. Not so long to wait, unless you're as anxious as me to see the results," he chuckled.

Suddenly, Garson felt very anxious. Mr. Rock had announced on Monday that everyone in his sixth-grade class would be doing class presentations of their science projects in eight weeks. *Oral* presentations. *In front of class.*

Eight weeks seemed far enough away on Monday. Now, on Wednesday, it did not. And after the slides arrived next week, some would need to be made into 8 x 10 prints. A key part of his project, and presentation, would be to match several of the new images to Mr. Rock's from forty years ago. Those photo pairs would tell a visual story to accompany the comparative measurements Garson took from the reference points to the glacier. The more the photos told, the less Garson would have to say. His heart thumped at the thought of speaking in front of his classmates. Classmates that included Billy Cribbs and Todd Ulander.

When the slides arrived and prints were made, he worried he wouldn't have time to put a great presentation together.

"Could we compare the measurements I took with the ones you took, before then?"

"In upcoming lessons, I'll be teaching how scientists analyze their data—the basics. You'll learn then how to compare the data you collected with mine."

Mr. Rock read Garson's expression, "This is your project. The more you do on your own, the more you'll learn."

"I know."

"If you run into a problem, ask and I'll get you back on track."

"Okay," Garson said trying to hide his disappointment. "Guess there's not much I can do til then."

"Science is a methodical process. It takes time to do it right. But there's plenty you can do before the slides arrive," he said, drawing Garson's eyes back to his.

"Like what?"

"Like writing. You can start drafting your assignment now. The details will fit in later. I know what you're thinking, you don't know yet how the photos and measurements will compare. Doesn't matter. Imagine how they will and write the story to fit it. You can always change the text and your conclusions later, if need be. By starting, you'll get the introduction, methods, and additional writing done. Not so much to do later," Mr. Rock hoisted his eyebrows.

Garson subconsciously frowned, twisting his lips toward one side of his mouth.

"This can be a great project. You've already done the hard

part, going to the glacier."

Garson nearly blurted out, "But I have to go back." He wanted to tell Mr. Rock so badly, but his teacher would surely ask why he needed to return to the mountain.

He didn't have a satisfactory answer, only that he needed to retrieve his bird book. He couldn't expect Mr. Rock to understand why he needed to climb the mountain again to retrieve a book. And he certainly would ask if Garson's mother had consented.

He shuddered inside at the thought of sharing the other reason—the one involving a talking goat and something about "special rocks." *Like Mr. Rock will buy that!* He might begin to wonder about Garson. Was he truthful? Perhaps a nut case? Even if he believed this tall tale, how could he expect Mr. Rock to back him up after Garson talked to his mom? His stomach churned.

That evening after dinner, Garson told his mom he wanted to call Toby. His mom looked up from the sink where she was rinsing dishes. "Oh?"

"We haven't talked in a long time."

"And you miss him," she replied as more of a statement than a question.

"I s'pose. I'll be in my room," he said as he grabbed the hand receiver from the base unit.

After learning that Toby was playing basketball and flag football, and sometimes fishing with his dad, Garson answered the question he expected would come. "Have you heard anything about your dad?"

After a pause, Garson simply said, "No." What else was there to say? At least Garson's loss was something Toby perhaps understood in some small way. With Toby's dad now in the command chain at Camp LeJeune, he hadn't been deployed for a few years. But other Marines their families knew had been sent to war zones. Dangerous places like Afghanistan, where his dad was, is, Garson corrected his thoughts. Everyone at LeJeune knew the same thing. Some of those deployed may not return. And if they did, not necessarily in the same way they'd gone to war.

In five years apart, both Garson and Toby had grown and changed. Change shaped by their environments, circumstances, and the interests each had developed. Still, there was a connection and Garson was glad to hear Toby's voice. Just to talk. But mostly, Garson felt the difference, even if he couldn't put his finger on it. There was a distance. Maybe because Toby spoke so much about his friends. He was way more outgoing. It made Garson hold back.

As the conversation lagged, he got up the nerve. After briefly explaining his trip to the glacier he said, "Now I need to go back to get a bird book. It was my dad's. He gave it to me. I don't know if I'll see him again. So it's kinda important."

"Well then go get it."

"I wish it was that easy," his voice trailed off. *How do I explain that she won't want me to go again? At least by myself. If dad was here ...* His throat tightened; his eyes grew moist. He hadn't talked to anyone about his dad this much in a while. Not even his mom.

"Sounds easy enough. You did it once. Just ask someone to go along if your mom insists."

Garson's heart sunk. This wasn't helping. Not helping at all. He couldn't tell Toby he didn't have a friend to ask along. And no way could he share with Toby his other reason for returning.

Buddy. Not in a million years! He wouldn't understand. Nobody could. They'd think he was crazy! And laugh at him. Garson hated being laughed at.

After ending the call, Garson sat on the edge of his bed with the phone in his hand. He was deflated. Empty feeling. And sad.

Chapter 17
Yes, A Small Man

Buddy and Roark were on the same page. At least she thought so as Roark flapped skyward. Shredded clouds skittered to the east as if fleeing the angry mass charging over Shining Mountain. Against this ominous backdrop, Roark circled overhead. Before sailing toward Goat Mountain, he performed a barrel roll and croaked her farewell.

Satisfied they'd meet again in seven sleeps, she trotted briskly southward. A pang of homesickness had squeezed her gut. Beyond the shoulder of Shining Mountain, she was heartened when she saw it. Goat Mountain. The place her band lived. Her home. Independent and adventurous as she was, emptiness engulfed her whenever she found herself alone. It was an internal struggle and conflict that stalked her. Like a tree unable to escape its shadow.

How Buddy envied Roark. With a tailwind blowing from the north, he'd soar to Goat Mountain in an hour, probably less. If only she could do that, she could see her band. *Yeah, right. A flying mountain goat. About as likely as a flying marmot!*

Instead, she wanted nothing more than to get back to Oreo. Before the snows came, they'd both journey home.

As she angled down the mountain, a nauseating feeling seized her. *What do I tell Oreo about today? How will she react?*

Oreo had no more contact with men than Buddy had. Only the brief and scary episode at the wasteland. *How will I ... how can I ... tell Oreo about Garson?*

I know. I'll tell her that Garson helped me. But that wasn't true, and it didn't explain why she needed to meet him again in seven sleeps.

Maybe ...

Nothing could explain why she arranged to rendezvous with him. Nothing but the truth.

Buddy had only felt this torn, and guilty, once before. That time involved Oreo too. It was after Roark told Buddy about the Legend of Shining Mountain and that she was chosen to be the new goat-Keeper of the Legend. After a day of internal turmoil, she told Oreo. She told her everything. She had to. If not, how could she live with herself? Besides, how else could she convince Oreo to join her on their perilous journey to Shining Mountain?

I don't know how to tell Oreo about Garson and ask to see him again. But she has always supported me and loved me. Hopefully, she will now too.

It wasn't far back to Oreo. Buddy almost wished it was farther. What had happened with Garson would be ... quite unbelievable. Even for Oreo who'd seen and heard many bizarre yet true things from Buddy over the past three months.

Suddenly, there was Oreo, jarring Buddy from her thoughts. She rose from her bed to greet Buddy. They reunited with customary affection: sniffing, nuzzling, and facial licking.

"I'm so glad you're back."

Buddy's heart was thumping, "I missed you so. Your shoulder looks better. Does it still hurt?"

"Hardly at all. I've been feeding more widely, working out the stiffness. It's getting stronger," she said with a lick of Buddy's ears. "Now tell me everything."

Everything. Okay. Here goes.

"I saw Tenanmouw again. And good thing too."

Oreo's ears perked straight up.

After Buddy described the rescue, Oreo said, "That's the second time he saved you from Gulo. It's too dangerous for you to wander the mountain alone."

"I suppose, but it's like Tenanmouw is watching over me. I can't explain it. He shows up when I need him. Just like Roark does."

"Or when Roark needs you. Not quite the same."

"But Roark saved me too."

True, Oreo reflected. *But then Roark recruited you to be the Legend Keeper. That's what propelled us on this journey into the unknown where none of our band had ever gone. Our lives would be simpler if we'd remained on Goat Mountain.*

These thoughts tormented Oreo most when she missed her mother, Spirit, and the others.

"I know. Roark did what he had to do. And you, my Buddy, did what you must do. Find how best you can contribute to the band."

"You're the one who told me that," Buddy laughed.

"And, so, I did. Of course, I had no idea my advice would lead us here," Oreo smiled as wide as a mountain goat can smile.

Buddy shared what she learned from Tenanmouw about Shining Mountain's food plants and winter cliffs.

"You've done well, as I knew you would. You're preparing to be a future leader and protector of the band."

Buddy wished she could end their conversation with this warm, fulfilled feeling inside. Of course, she couldn't.

"There's more to tell you. Something happened on my way back."

"Let's lay on this bed of soft sedges while we talk." Oreo gingerly dropped to her front knees, then folded her legs beneath her. "Now what is it? What else happened to you?"

"I met someone new."

"A goat from the Shining Mountain band?"

"No."

Haltingly at first, Buddy related her encounter with Garson. As she did, she watched Oreo's uneasiness grow.

Finally, Oreo leapt to her feet, as if she had two perfectly healthy shoulders.

"A man? Remember how the wasteland man chased and frightened you!"

"I know. He frightened me terribly. But this one was different. Even Roark thought so."

"Roark?"

"He showed up after I helped the boy get unstuck."

"*Boy?*"

"Roark called him a small man, but Garson called himself a boy. I think that's the same as me being a kid—until I get older."

Oreo's head was spinning. Her band lived in remote wilderness. They didn't come in contact with men, or boys.

"You *talked* to him, like you do to Roark and Maurice? He told you his *name*?" Oreo stammered.

Buddy hoped to convince her of something that only Oreo might believe. If she tried explaining this to others in her band, they'd laugh Buddy off a cliff!

"He told me stuff about the glacier and about how things are changing on the mountains."

Before Oreo could interject a parade of questions, Buddy jumped to the main point.

"Garson is coming back in seven sleeps. And I want to see him then to find out if he can help us."

Oreo shook her head. "No more. We can't trust men. Look what they did to the forest. They made it a wasteland. Other men may be the same, including this one." Oreo stamped a front foot.

Buddy was shaken. Despite knowing her adoptive mother wouldn't be keen on this, Buddy didn't expect such defiance.

"You're not dealing with marmots or ravens or owls here. Men are a different kind of animal. We know little about them, and what we do know is alarming."

Buddy was lost. It was as if she was following a ledge that became narrower and narrower. And then it ended, with no space to turn around, no room for a walkover. *How can I make her see what my instincts tell me? Garson could help our band.*

"You know how Spirit says it takes goats working together to make a band? Watching for predators and finding the best food patches."

"What are you leading up to?"

"What happened earlier was like that ... with the boy, Garson."

"What's *that* got to do with our band of goats?" Oreo snapped.

"Garson needed my help. It's why I could talk to him, just like when TS needed my help, or when I needed Maurice and Whodare's help, and we could talk."

Oreo was beginning to calm down. The crest of hair along her back was no longer standing on end.

"I've learned so much from you and Spirit," said Buddy. "But now our band is in trouble at Goat Mountain. Our numbers have dwindled. And I know it worries you both."

"What are you trying to tell me?"

"Our band needs help and soon the Shining Mountain band will too. Mystic knows it. She is wise too." Buddy took a deep breath. "I believe Garson can help us. He wants to. He's not like wasteland man. He wants to protect our land from the changes that you and Spirit see happening."

"And just *how* could he help?"

Buddy paused, wishing she had a good answer. "I don't know yet. But in seven sleeps I'll find out."

Oreo's expression softened. "Buddy, you are so different from the rest of us. You think about the future more than any goat I've known. Including Spirit. You also have an unnerving penchant to trust others."

"I only want to contribute to the band."

Oreo couldn't avoid smiling. The tension finally broke, which called for a heavy dose of grooming. Tongues slurped each other's face and neck, as they shared their deep love for each other.

"In seven sleeps, you say?"

"Yes. I'm supposed to meet him at the glacier."

"I've always trusted your instincts and yearnings. I've not regretted I did. But this is your biggest gamble yet. My gut tells me there's little to be gained, and maybe much to lose. We can't know the real motive of the man. Mostly I'm worried he may harm you. And Tenanmouw may not magically appear to protect you."

The harsh edge left her voice. "Still, I'm going to trust you, once again."

"I'll be alright, Oreo. He seems very gentle. Besides, Roark will protect me if I need it."

"And how could Roark protect you from a man?"

"You've seen that wicked beak of his!"

"He's still just a croaking bird. No, I will come with you."

"But that might scare Garson away."

"I won't be looking over your shoulder, only keeping a watchful eye from a distance. A trek to the glacier will be a good test of my shoulder's progress."

And so the deal was struck.

Chapter 18
How to Ask Her

Far, far down the mountain, at the edge of the town of Pinewood, at the end of a gravel road, a log cabin nestled beside a woodland of pine and fir. Inside the cabin, Garson too was counting the days, I mean sleeps. Much was on his mind. He couldn't recall being in such turmoil, with so many things banging inside his head. He remembered his dad used to say, "When you've got too much to do, do one thing, then another, and another. Soon all will be done."

He was tempted to begin writing his science report first, like Mr. Rock advised. Garson really disliked writing. Starting with that task was a sure sign he was avoiding the most important thing on the list. *I've gotta talk to mom about Saturday. I've gotta ask her.*

Thursday after school, Garson was at his computer when he heard the front door open and close. He heard her handbag and groceries land on the dining room table. No sense waiting.

"Hi mom. How was work?"

Lucy took note of the cheery face greeting her. "Fine, Garson. You seem especially happy. Something good happen at school?"

"Nothin' special."

She knew something was up. But what?

He snatched the two bags of groceries, took them to the kitchen and began putting them away.

"Thank you, honey."

He really disliked when she called him honey, but he rarely said so. Besides, he wanted her in the best of moods when he made the ask.

They chatted through dinner. More than usual. While she cleared the table, he served up bowls of vanilla ice cream.

When she rejoined him at the table, she said warmly, "This is so nice of you."

C'mon Garson, you can't wait all night. Ask her. He cleared his throat and looked straight at her.

"Mom, there's something I've gotta ask you. Could you take me to the Lupine Lake trailhead on Saturday?"

"Whatever for?"

He fidgeted in his chair. He forced himself not to look down—a sure giveaway that he was concealing something.

"I need to go back to the glacier."

"Garson, not again. You did your study. Why would you go back?"

"You know the bird book dad gave me?"

"Of course."

"Well, I left it there. I set it down and left it by the glacier."

"When did you realize that?"

"A while ago. I've been wanting to ask you, but I knew you wouldn't want me to go back."

"Hiking up there is dangerous. Look how you hurt your leg the last time."

"I know. But that's because I was hurrying ... the measurements and photographs took so long."

"Honey, I know you treasure that gift from your father. But I will buy you another one just like it."

"It wouldn't be the same. It wouldn't be the one Dad gave me."

She reached across the table. Reluctantly, Garson took her

hand. Somehow it felt like surrendering.

"I know. But I don't want you hiking back up the mountain again. Your book is not worth risking your life. Besides, who would go with you?"

It was just a book, hardly worth the risk of an accident in her eyes. It's what any parent would say. But the book wasn't the only reason he needed to return. Garson felt stuck. *Am I going to have to tell her? How do I explain I've got a meeting with a goat ... and a raven?*

This would be tough, but he had to do it. Buddy would be waiting for him; and he really wanted to know the secrets she held about the mountain.

"Dad made notes in the book. About places we saw birds. It means a lot to me."

Garson paused. His mother wiped her eyes with the back of her hand before the tears spilled down her cheeks. Garson did the same.

Neither spoke for a bit. A stalemate.

"There's something else. Another reason I need to go back."

She straightened in her chair.

"You're probably not going to believe this. Sometimes I still have trouble. But it's the truth."

"What? What else, Garson?"

"When I was coming down from the glacier and fell, something happened. I guess I yelled out when I banged my shin. Someone came to help."

Lucy was leaning forward now, back stiff as a board, hands clasped on the table. Her blue eyes big as ping pong balls.

"Someone? Who?"

Garson swallowed hard. He wished he'd thought this little talk through earlier. He'd only shared it with his dad. Garson knew he'd listen. He'd understand. He always did. Even though he wasn't really there, it still helped.

Now he dug deep. "Her name is Buddy."

Lucy's eyes grew bigger.

"She's a mountain goat."

Garson saw her knuckles turn white like when she drove up the Forest Service road last Saturday. He thought her head might explode.

"What?"

Garson recapped his encounter with Buddy: how she helped free his foot, told him about her goat band, and how they talked about the melting glacier. He skipped the talking raven.

Except for some gasps and an occasional "Oh my," Lucy didn't interrupt. Garson assumed she was in shock.

"That's why I need to go back on Saturday. I promised Buddy. She's going to tell me some important stuff about the mountain. I think it might help with my science project."

Garson exhaled a deep breath. He sat back in his chair, eyes landing on his empty bowl.

"Wait, wait a minute. We need to back up. I ... I don't know where to begin!"

Garson's stomach was doing flip-flops.

"Garson, my dear son. You know I love you more than anything. And I want you to feel you can tell me anything, like troubles you're having at school with those bullies, or when you're especially missing your dad. But ... this is so hard to believe," she paused. "How do you know this was a mountain goat?"

"I know what they look like from my research on glaciers. They live up there."

"Okay, you've seen pictures of them. But are you *sure* you really saw one? And how do you know his name?" She shook her head slowly. "You know you took a bad fall up there. Are you sure you weren't unconscious and imagined all this?"

"Buddy is a she, not a he. She told me her name and everything else. It's real, mom. It really happened."

Lucy slowly shook her head in doubt.

"And I can prove it. Here's a tuft of her hair."

She took the silky tuft and rolled it between her fingers. "But you could have found it on the ground."

"You have to believe me. I'm not crazy, even if what happened sounds like it."

Lucy rose from her chair, walked around the table, and threw her arms around Garson. He heard her sobs and felt her tears course onto his cheek. He hugged her back, as best he could. She was squeezing him so tightly, he felt paralyzed.

She let go, wiped her face on the sleeve of her shirt and returned to her chair. "I have so many questions, but I'll ask just one, for now. Is there any reason you'd tell me this story other than it's true?"

"No mom. It's true. I've been wanting to tell you all week. That's why I called Toby. I planned to tell him, then ask how he thought I should tell you."

"You told Toby?" she exclaimed.

"Nah. It didn't work out. But I needed to tell someone, and most of all you."

"I should probably dial the mental health hotline, but I believe you. This story is too far-fetched to make up. How you could talk to a mountain goat ... I've never even seen one." She waggled her head. "I don't understand."

"Me neither. It just happened."

"Just happened, like falling off a log," she feigned a weak laugh. "Okay. I'm going to *assume* this mountain goat can keep track of time. She'll know when your *meeting* on Saturday rolls around."

"She knows it's in seven sleeps. I mean days. Don't ask me how."

Lucy closed her eyes, tight, then looked at Garson for a few seconds.

"Well, this sure sounds important to you. Otherwise, you wouldn't have gone through the stress of telling me. And maybe giving me a heart attack." She smiled.

"It's real important, mom."

"Just one thing. Why couldn't this goat ..."

"Buddy."

"Yes, Buddy, have told you her secrets when you were there last Saturday?"

"She wanted to. Then I looked at my watch and saw how late I was going to be, getting back to the car. You were waiting and I knew you'd be worried."

Again, she held back tears. She slipped into the bathroom for some tissues to blot her eyes and a good blow of her nose. *I'm going to look a sight tomorrow morning at work,* she thought while looking in the mirror.

"Sorry," she dabbed her eyes and exhaled a sigh. "Oh Garson. What would I do without you?"

Garson saw her curl her mouth in a way that made her look like a schoolgirl.

"Now we're right back where we were last Saturday. Except now, we know I can't hike up there with you. Who can?"

Garson fidgeted in his chair. He looked at the table, "No one. But it doesn't matter."

"Of course, it matters."

"Mom, I have to do this alone. Buddy trusts me, and ..." He almost slipped and told her about Roark, who also wasn't crazy about this get-together. Roark surely wouldn't want another human to crash the party.

"And what?" she cocked her head.

"Well, she trusts me. And who knows what might have happened if she didn't help get my foot unstuck."

Garson searched for something conclusive to make his case. Nothing came to him.

"If someone else went with me, if there was someone else, what would they think? And what if they didn't keep it a secret? Spread it around school. I'd have to move."

"Well, that's a little dramatic. But I see your point."

She ran her fingers through her hair and said, "I'm exhausted. Let me think about this. We'll talk tomorrow."

She smiled her schoolgirl smile again. "Don't worry. I still love you."

"I love you too."

Only then did Garson feel like an 800-pound gorilla had hopped off his shoulders. This time he walked around the table and hugged his mom.

In the morning, she made Garson his favorite. Pancakes with an egg on top, drowned in syrup.

Mrs. Strangewalker watched him as he ate. She had resolved her dilemma, except for some details. She had asked herself again and again last night, "What would John say?" She knew. He'd say to trust him. "Let the boy take chances. Trial and error is the best teacher." The error part is what Lucy was having trouble with.

"I thought about our conversation last night. In fact, I thought about it much of the night. Can you tell?" She made a face that exaggerated the lines on her forehead.

Garson laughed. A chunk of pancake erupted from his mouth onto the table. They both laughed.

She shook her head. "No one could make up a story like that. I know you've wanted a dog. Instead, you found a pet mountain goat."

They both laughed again until Garson nearly choked on his pancakes. After he wiped the napkin across his face, he said, "Not a pet. Maybe more like a silent partner in my science project."

"I like that," Lucy nodded approvingly, eyebrows raised.

"Okay. I can drive you to the trailhead, but I can't wait for you. I have a segment to film Saturday. Something I can't put off. What time will you get back to the trailhead?"

"Because I don't have all the measurements and pictures to take, it shouldn't take as long. Last time I said five o'clock."

"Yes, and you didn't show up until almost seven."

"I know, but I only had the accident cuz I was rock hopping, trying to hurry."

She cringed at the thought of him falling.

"Not doin' *that* again," he gestured. "I should be back by three, four at the latest."

"I'm not sure if I can get away by then. Maybe Mr. Rock could meet you."

"That would be pretty cool! I'll ask him today."

Chapter 19
In the Woods

Friday, September 20

Before biking to school, Garson checked the internet weather forecast. Bummer! A storm system was building on the West Coast. It would arrive sometime this weekend, most likely Sunday, but the exact timing was iffy.

Adding to his angst, Garson was dreading another day of torment by Billy and Todd. He tried his best to avoid them. But they were in some of his classes, including science. At least he didn't have to sit near the creep crew.

As Garson headed for English, his first class on Friday, they intercepted him. "Saw you sucking up to Doc Rock," Cribbs mocked. "Workin' on your grade, Straaaaange?" Ulander yukked.

Avoiding eye contact, Garson ducked past them. Geez!

At his desk, in the refuge of the classroom, he tried for a moment to do what his mom always said, "Try to look for the best in people." *Maybe they're bored and not really creeps. Nah, not likely.* He was just thankful they hadn't seen him talking to Kira, the red-haired volcano maker.

At the end of Friday's science class, Garson tarried until the other students exited the room. "Mr. Rock, can I ask you something?"

"Ahhh, Garson. Of course."

He explained his intention to hike back to the glacier to retrieve his book, how his mom could take him, but she might not return in time to meet him. "Could you maybe pick me up?"

Mr. Rock knitted his bushy eyebrows, "I assume you plan on hiking alone, since you didn't say 'we.' Your mother's okay with that?"

"I've done it once. This time there are no measurements or pictures to take. I've even got the trail marked already with flags."

"If you must go back, I'd feel better if you went with someone—maybe a classmate."

"No one would want to. And they probably couldn't keep up anyway."

Mr. Rock's expression mellowed. "If your mother is good with this, then yes, I'll meet you at the trailhead. I'll call her this evening."

"Thanks, Mr. Rock."

Spinning to leave the classroom, he reveled, *Yes, it's gonna happen.*

"Garson."

He pivoted in the doorway, "What, Mr. Rock?"

"That book must be very important to you."

Garson nodded.

He sensed something in his teacher's voice, something probing. *Does he suspect there's more to my return to the glacier?*

Garson pedaled his bike like a T. rex was chasing him. Upright, he drove the pedals furiously, only braking lightly for the two stop signs along the route home. His heart pounded like he was running. *Running.* It struck him; *I haven't been for a run in a week.* Only running could calm the turmoil inside his head.

He skidded his bike onto the lawn and burst through the door to tell his mom Mr. Rock could meet him. The house was empty. Some days she couldn't get off work before Garson got home after school.

He tossed his backpack onto the bed, changed into running shorts and shoes, drank a glass of water, and was out the door. Garson loved that in minutes, he could be running in the forest at the foot of the mountain. It was "his woods," the place where he spotted wildlife and felt his legs propel him through the trees. A place to chill out. A place where he dared allow himself to think about his dad. Sometimes picture the two of them together.

As he ran, a jumble of images and voices materialized. His tormenters, Billy and Todd. The anger and powerlessness they made him feel. Disappointment over his phone call with Toby. *If he's my best friend, why did he seem so different?* Today's conversations with his mom and Mr. Rock. Anticipation about tomorrow. *Will Buddy really be there to meet me?* How to write up his science project. His dread of the oral class presentation. And most of all, missing his dad. *I wish I could talk to him about this stuff.*

He pumped his legs faster and faster, barely aware of his surroundings or where he was going. Abruptly he pulled to a stop, gasping for breath. Then everything began to slow down ... his breathing, his thinking, the chaos inside. The forest came into focus. Then each stately tree ... long-needled Ponderosa pines with puzzle-like bark and tightly needled Douglas firs. He felt like an interloper in an empire of ancients.

In silence, studying the trees, an eerie feeling crept over him. *They're watching me.*

It was like last Saturday while trying to get his boot unstuck. The same unnerving feeling of being watched. Then, as it turned out, by a mountain goat.

Garson turned his head, half expecting to see eyes bugging from an ancient, furrowed trunk. Unlike the Ents in Tolkien's *Lord of the Rings*, no gawking eyes and arm-waving limbs materialized. Instead, as he scoured the branches and underbrush. *Whoa! There's an owl staring at me!*

Perched on a branch eye-level to Garson, the owl was no bigger than a coke can. Had it not blinked its golden eyes, he might have missed its gray-brown form.

Of all the times he'd run in these woods, this was a first. *How many times has an owl like this seen me; and I haven't seen it?*

He noted its field markings—lack of ear tufts, streaked breast, and pint size. *I'll look it up when I get home.* Instantly, he remembered his field guide was at the glacier.

Garson turned to discover if anything else was watching. Nothing he could see. When he turned back, the owl took flight.

Garson followed, feeling the joy of hurtling off-trail through the trees. Each time he lost sight of the owl's gliding figure, he stopped to study the forest ahead. Each time, a pair of hollow notes— "Took, Took"—led him to the owl before it winged on. At last, the owl settled onto a branch.

Alone in a place he had never been, he felt supersensitized to his surroundings. He saw, really *saw*, the unspoiled beauty of the forest—not just the trees, but everything from the forest floor, to standing snags laced with lime-green lichens and woodpecker holes, to boughs knitted against the cloud-studded sky. It all fit magically. Yet something starkly stood out, discordant with the rest. Vivid red rings.

In front of Garson, dozens and dozens of them hung at eye level. Well, not exactly hung. Spray-painted around the trunks of the largest pines and firs were rings of red. Behind him there were none. To his right and left was a dividing line, as obvious as a fence, between a forest of painted and unpainted trees.

Fastened to a post, was a yellow sign. He walked to it and read the black lettering, “PROPERTY BOUNDARY National Forest land behind this sign.”

Wording on a metal sign nailed to a nearby Douglas fir, read “Cutting Unit Boundary.”

Cutting. That could only mean one thing.

A prickle of realization ran down Garson’s spine. *The owl. It led me here. Why?*

Garson spun back toward where the owl was perched. Vanished. There no more.

I’ve gotta find out about this when I get home.

Angling back down the slope, he intercepted the trail. He beat feet home ... with a new worry muddling his mind.

Chapter 20

Return to Shining Mountain

Saturday, September 21

At 7:30, the Subaru was bouncing back up the US Forest Service road to Lupine Lake trailhead. This time, Mrs. Strangewalker was dressed for her day job, not for a hike. Along with everything else he needed, Garson had stuffed in his black daypack an extra fleece top, gloves, and stocking hat. "You know, in case," his mom had said.

She got no argument from Garson. He'd seen the forecast. Despite the bluebird skies this morning, a storm was barreling toward Shining Mountain. Winter weather conditions were predicted for the weekend, starting late today. Garson tried to blot the image of a mountain pelted by snow from his mind.

As she pulled into the vacant trailhead parking area, Lucy said, "Well, here we are, my mountain goat son."

"Yeah, we made it again without losing the exhaust system," Garson smiled back.

"You know, you can still change your mind."

"No way," Garson quipped. "I've got an important meeting to go to."

"Me too, but mine's with some pencil pushers, not a mountain goat."

They both laughed. Lucy placed her hand on Garson's cheek,

her expression turned sober. “You’ve got my cell phone. It’s charged up, but you should probably leave it turned off to save the battery. At least til you get to the glacier.”

Garson nodded.

“I’ll be with the crew today, including Amanda. Here’s her cell number.” She handed him a folded paper. “Her number’s also in the phone’s contact list, under Perkins.”

“Okay,” he said, feeling anxious to hit the trail.

“Just to be sure, leave a message at the house too ...” She caught herself before the words “if you need help” slipped out.

“I know, mom.”

She detected the irritation in his voice.

“Sure you’re alright? Got everything you need?”

“I’m sure. I better get going.”

She leaned across the seat and flung her arms around him. “Please, please be careful.”

He nodded.

“Oh, do you have Mr. Rock’s number?”

“Yeah,” he pulled a scrap of paper from his pocket and showed her.

She resisted the urge to tell him to keep it in a safe place.

“Hey, before you go, how about a selfie of us in front of the sign?”

“Okay,” he said with a groan she detected.

As she snapped the photo of them posing in front of the trailhead sign, Lucy said, “We didn’t do this the last time.”

He saw her face tighten.

“Love you, Mom. Thanks again for trusting me.”

“I love you too,” she replied as he strode toward the trail.

As she pulled away, Garson waved. He plucked the altimeter from his pack and adjusted the elevation setting to the known elevation at the trailhead. Then he struck out at a fast pace.

The temperature was cool, perfect for hiking. He was soon at Lupine Lake, then the meadow where the trail ended. He hesitated at the old fire ring, trying to spot the eagle. He recalled the agonizing decision he and his mom made here last Saturday.

Following the faint game trail, now festooned with pink flags, his legs surged up the slope. Exhilaration filled him, pure happiness from the self-reliance of exploring this wilderness on his own. *I'm really doing this again.* With thoughts of mountain goats and glaciers swirling in his head, he pushed upward as if he'd trekked this path a hundred times. Bursting with excitement, but also doubts about whether she'd really be there, he was barely aware of his progress.

At the aspen grove, he snacked on dried apricots and gorp. With less gear to carry this time, he brought three quarts of water and drank liberally from one of the bottles.

When he broke from the last of the whitebark pines at mid-morning, he wasn't tired from the climb. How could he be? Once through the knotted drifts of krumholtz, only alpine meadow lay between him and the glacier. *I'll soon see Buddy, I hope.* His skin was tingling.

Seeing her would prove what happened last Saturday was real.

He scanned the alpine searching for the boulder where they'd met. He thought of it as the Trust Rock. Its shape and patterned green and orange lichens were etched in his mind. The photograph wasn't needed.

Before he spotted her ivory ball of fluff far up the mountain, a solitary raven croaked overhead, "Toc, Toc, Toc." It banked and soared toward the goat. Garson's heart thumped. His legs pumped.

Getting nearer, it sure looked like Buddy. Besides, she didn't run away. Wouldn't any other mountain goat, like other wild animals, flee from a hard-charging human?

When he reached her, Garson could feel the smile stretched across his face. For a few seconds, they stared at each other in wonder.

Buddy hopped to a nearer rock and said, "I'm glad you came back."

Garson squeezed the Swiss Army knife and confessed, "I didn't know if I would really see you again."

"Why, didn't you think I'd be here?"

"Because ..." a number of reasons shot through his head, but he just said, "because you're a mountain goat and I'm a human. I don't think this happens very often."

Buddy thought about this for a bit. "Hu-man? Aren't you a small man, a boy?"

"You're right. I'm a boy, a not-grown-up human. Humans are different kinds of animals than you and Roark."

"Maybe we're not so different. Not if we both think what's happening on Shining Mountain, and Goat Mountain is bad. But what are you doing here that can help?"

Her words struck Garson as direct, almost a challenge. Still, he remained mystified. *It's as if I'm talking with a person.*

Chapter 21
Strange Rocks

Walking side by side to the glacier, Buddy quizzed him. Questions to satisfy her curiosity and to probe Roark's fears about the boy. What did he know about the glacier melting? Why was it important? Questions about his teacher? What could they do about the changes happening? And—in deference to Roark's apprehension—are more men coming to Shining Mountain?

As they treaded up the yellowed meadow, strewn with gray granite rock, Buddy spotted Oreo above her on the glacier. She was elated Oreo had gained the elevation so fast. *Her shoulder must be much better.*

She was careful not to alert Garson that they were being watched.

Not far from the ice, Buddy stopped. Garson waited for Buddy to speak. Instead, she looked at her feet, where the silvery gray granite of the mountain's bedrock ended as if halted by some mythical force.

"Why did you stop here?" Garson asked.

"You remember me asking, 'Did you see the rocks' when we met seven sleeps ago?"

"I've been thinking about it ever since. I don't know what you meant. Up here there are rocks everywhere. More than any place I've ever been."

"Look," Buddy gestured toward their feet.

As if an image had snapped into focus, Garson saw the mountain's changed identity. A split personality like the horizon splitting the earth from sky.

"I didn't *see* this before. One kind of rock where we've been, then this tan rock here."

Looking left then right, the abrupt change in the mountain's building blocks continued like water meeting a beach. "And it keeps going," he exclaimed.

Buddy nodded at his reaction.

"Are ... are they just a different color?"

Recalling how Tenanmouw had ordered her to taste the rock, Buddy said, "More than that. Taste it."

"What?"

"Lick both kinds of rock, the gray and then the tan."

Garson's forehead furrowed. His nose scrunched up. "Why?"

"You'll find out, and better than I can tell you."

Kneeling down, he gave her a sideways look of dismay before licking the rough, gray granite. It didn't taste like much. Maybe a little metallic.

He gave Buddy another glance, half expecting her to break into goat laughter, however that sounded. No sign of jesting crossed her face. He swiveled on his knees, lowered his head, and slid his tongue across the smooth, tan stone.

"Yuk! It tastes bitter."

"Bitter like limestone," Buddy knowingly nodded.

What? Garson looked around him. *I've read a lot about mountains, but I've never read about this. How's it possible that there's limestone here on top when the rest of the mountain is granite?!*

As Garson rose to his feet, a sudden whoosh of wings nearly sent him sprawling from fright.

"Thanks for dropping in, Roark," Buddy quipped as the raven folded his wings and settled on a block of granite.

"And maybe not a moment too soon. Seems you're about to tell all to small man."

"Remember, we agreed to see if Garson could help us."

"Still don't trust him. He may have caused you no bodily harm, but his intentions may do something worse!"

Garson was back at the tennis match, watching the two caw and bleat. *I can't even tell if they like each other.*

"Did you tell him about the Legend?" Roark croaked.

"No."

"Well don't. Instead, find out how he intends to help."

When Buddy asked, Garson explained his science project as best he could. He related the melting of the glacier to the warming of the planet—clearly a foreign concept to a small goat living on a mountaintop. Garson did his best.

Rather than trying to explain how the burning of fossil fuels was causing the warming, he simply said, "The warming is going to get worse."

"You're sure?"

"Well, the scientists are all sure. They're the ones who know the most about this. And they know how it can be stopped."

"What's he saying?" Roark squawked.

"Wait a minute. I'll tell you when he's done," Buddy said more sharply than she'd wished.

"But stopping it's a big problem. The biggest problem is convincing people—other humans—to change what they're doing. Maybe I can help with that," Garson added hesitantly.

Mmmm. Buddy narrowed her eyes. She understood much about the lives of the other animals where she lived: marmots, eagles, deer, voles, owls, ravens—she glanced fondly at Roark—and others. *I don't know anything about these humans. But it sounds like they aren't concerned about the return of the Great Warming. Maybe because they don't know the Legend. Maybe it's like when I had to convince Oreo and she had to convince Spirit of needing to go to Shining Mountain where things would be better for us.*

"Some of us see the problem too," Buddy replied.

"You do?" Garson asked.

Roark could hardly contain himself, hopping from one foot to the other, fluffing his feathers, and squawking.

"You're going to scare him, Roark," Buddy bleated. "Okay, I'll tell you. Garson wants to know why we're worried about the Great Warming. I don't see how I can explain it without telling him about the Shining Mountain Legend. To make it clear."

Roark protested, "No. The Legend is entrusted to goats and ravens. It's not to be shared with others, and certainly not with men. We Legend Keepers must honor our obligation."

Buddy took a deep breath in frustration. "But what good is this story if we don't put it to use?"

"I've told you before, the Legend is not just a story. It honors our origins and how we survived."

"Exactly. A long line of raven-Keepers and goat-Keepers didn't preserve the Legend of Shining Mountain because it's a nice story about our past. They did it—and you and I are doing it—because its message is about more than the past. I think it warns of the future. We can benefit from that knowledge if we choose."

Silence.

Roark fixed a steely-eyed gaze on Buddy, "And how do you propose to do that by telling this boy?"

Buddy was ready with her answer, "Garson's the only human who's come here. I believe he's come for a reason ... to help us. Maybe he can convince the other humans to stop the warming."

Roark was flustered, confused, and angry all at once. *She continues to challenge our traditions, the code by which we've always done things. Yet it was I who chose her to become the next goat-Keeper of the Legend.* Ruffling of feathers. *Drat! What was I thinking?*

After scratching his head with a toe, he uttered a single "Rurruk" of resignation. "I have trusted your judgment before. Call me daffy, I will again. But make sure he gives you his word—no others like him come here."

"Thanks, Roark. I'll tell him."

While the two were jabbering, Garson unshouldered his pack and retrieved the phone. He took two photos: one where the granite and limestone met near his feet, another toward the glacier. He hesitated, then snapped a third of Buddy and Roark. A stab of guilt cut him, as if he'd stolen something.

With Roark's acquiescence, Buddy related to Garson the hardships harming her band. "Our numbers are shrinking. I'm the only kid who survived this year. Only ten remain in our band."

"Where are the others?"

"On Goat Mountain. Our home."

"I remember you telling me that you came here looking for a better place to live."

"Yes, a place where our food plants don't dry up in summer. A place with plenty of snow to keep us cool on hot days. Our matriarch, Spirit, is wise. She says summers are getting warmer. But she doesn't want to leave our home."

"What made you choose to come to this place? Did your band live here before?"

Buddy knew the only way to answer this was to explain the Legend. *Will he believe me?*

Avoiding Roark's stare, she said, "I'm going to tell you

something not shared with animals like you. Something sacred to goats and ravens. It's our Legend. The Legend of Shining Mountain."

Garson felt his skin prickle.

"If I tell you, can you keep the Legend a secret?"

"Yes ... I will," Garson answered, feeling Roark's eyes hot on his face. "I promise."

"Good. Long ago a great peril descended on our home. The Great Warming. It brought hardship, as I said. Goats and other animals, even ravens, suffered."

Garson's eyes flashed to Roark. "Even ravens?"

"It's complicated. Just know that the fortunes of ravens and goats are forever linked. Roark is the one who told me. And he knows better than any other." *Except, of course, Battenmouw and Tenanmouw, but there's no way I'm explaining all of that.*

Garson frowned dubiously. "This is from a Legend?"

"The Legend of Shining Mountain. This is what Roark and I know to be true, like all of our ancestors did."

Why not? Garson considered. *Humans do the same. We believe in legends and other stuff that maybe we can't prove.*

"To provide us a refuge from the Great Warming's hardships, Shining Mountain was built."

"Built?! What d'ya mean?"

"I know. When Roark first told me, I found it hard to believe too."

"You mean, *built?* Like someone made it higher than what was here?" Garson waved an arm.

"Yes."

"How? How could that happen?"

"How is not of importance right now. I know it's true and that's how our band escaped the Great Warming's hardships back then. Now the warming is returning. We see the evidence."

Garson rubbed the jackknife in his pocket. *So this is why Shining Mountain is so special, and important, to Buddy.*

"I thought our band would be safe here on Shining Mountain. Now I'm not so sure." Buddy's eyes narrowed. "Mystic, the matriarch of the Shining Mountain band, foresees troubles even on this high mountain with its snow and ice. Our bands have nowhere else to go."

A pang of sadness swept Garson. *Glaciers and goats are alike. Both are found high on mountains and need the cold. If glaciers disappear, might mountain goats too?*

By now Roark was in a tizzy. Feathers were fleeing his flapping wings.

"What are you telling him?"

"Why I came here. And how the Legend foreshadowed a return of the Great Warming."

Roark let loose a pitiful squawk. *Oh for the days when I was in control.*

"Don't worry. I'm giving him the short version. No mention of Mouw and Ten."

"You're sure."

"Of course. I want him to believe me, and not think I'm full of locoweed." A smile creased the corners of her mouth.

Buddy and Roark scrutinized Garson as he spoke.

"I don't know a lot about how mountains form ... only what Mr. Rock, my teacher has told us. And what I've read."

Read? This brought a puzzled look to Buddy's face.

"But I don't think mountains are built. How can you be sure Shining Mountain was built?"

"You already know the answer."

"I do?" Garson's jaw hung slack.

"You've seen the evidence," Buddy nodded her head. "It's at your feet. And from here to the glacier."

Garson's eyes followed hers. Everywhere he looked, the limestone slabs exhibited an intricate design, side by side and end to end. It was like he'd rotated the focus ring on binoculars to sharpen a blurry image.

"I didn't see this before. From here to the glacier, the rock is in a regular pattern," he paused. "Like someone laid it here!"

Buddy nodded and tipped her head a little higher. "This is what I wanted you to see. It was laid here."

Garson's wide-eyed expression spoke volumes. Despite not understanding a word he said, Garson's look was as obvious to Roark as a bolt of lightning. The boy knew he was seeing a wonder. Something defying explanation. No expression of doubt.

I'm not going to read this in any book, Garson realized.

"This is way more than a science project," he murmured.

Chapter 22
The Parting

A breeze sprung from the northwest. Enough to send a shiver through Garson. Ragged fingers had thrust from a menacing cloudbank. They clawed Shining Mountain. The sun, which should have been near its zenith, had vanished without a trace. Garson checked his watch—shortly after noon.

"I've gotta get going," he said reluctantly. "I have to get my book."

Another puzzled look from Buddy. *Book?*

Dreamlike as it was, this time with Buddy felt like a priceless gift. A bond, however tenuous, had forged between Garson and this amazing animal.

"When will I see you again?"

"I leave soon to join my band on Goat Mountain," she said eagerly. "I may not return to Shining Mountain until the winter snows melt."

The impact of her words settled in Garson's gut. "You taught me a lot. About how you and your band live up here. And what's changing."

Buddy gazed toward the glacier. She could make out the top of Oreo's head. When her eyes returned to Garson, she wistfully said, "I believe the Legend foretells a return of the Great Warming. You too believe this is true."

Not as a question, rather her words struck Garson as an

indisputable judgment.

"Kraaa, kraaa." Roark prepared to take flight. After he and Buddy exchanged some caws and bleats, Buddy turned back to Garson. "We want to know; will you stop the warming?"

The innocence and pleading in her eyes reinforced how mountain goats, like other living things, were victims of forces far beyond their control. Garson guessed the truth. These animals living on islands in the sky were in danger. And most people were ignorant of it.

Garson's heart was racing. *It's impossible. I'm just a sixth-grader with a science project and a fear of talking in front of class. How can I stop the climate from warming?*

He swallowed hard and said, "Buddy, I will try, I really will, to help keep your home safe."

Buddy didn't respond. She didn't have to. The gratitude in her eyes was enough.

He squeezed the jackknife in his pocket, hesitated, and said, "Before I leave, can I touch you?"

At that moment Roark flapped skyward. With a soothing, "Cur-ruk," he left Buddy alone and unsure how to respond to Garson's request.

Buddy blinked, "Why?"

"It's what humans do ... when we care about someone."

"You mean some mountain goat?"

"Yes," Garson smiled.

Buddy nodded slightly.

Garson stepped closer, stretched out his hand, and softly, almost imperceptibly, touched the wavy fleece on her face. As his fingertips lingered there, the two looked at each other the way the closest of friends might. Wonderment filled him.

Then Buddy stepped away, turned, and trotted off.

Watching her bound across the meadow, Garson remembered

something he'd read. How forbears of mountain goats came from Asia to North America during the Great Ice Age. Buddy's ancestors had roamed this very mountain since the great continental glaciers yielded enough land for alpine habitats to support life. This was their domain. *The goats belong here, and the mountains belong to the mountain goats. For how much longer?*

Garson would never forget Buddy's words, "Will you stop the warming?"

Chapter 23
Book and Bird

A gust buffeted Garson. From his pack, he pulled on the extra fleece top, zip-up rain jacket, and gloves. He tugged a stocking cap over his ears in place of his Audubon logo baseball cap. All but the purple jacket was black.

Plodding north toward the reference points, the first wind-driven snow pellets began stinging his face. He lowered his head. With the jacket's drawcord cinched tight, his upper body was almost hermetically sealed. His legs were a different story. Denim cargo pants did little to blunt the wind.

It took only fifteen minutes to reach the little stream he remembered tumbling past reference marker number one. His heart quickened. *What if the pink surveyor's tape blew off the rebar?* When he spotted the flagging faithfully snapping in the gale, he felt a rush of relief. But only for a moment. *How am I gonna find the book?* The ground was now glazed in white.

In his mind, Garson pictured the spot where he'd filled his water bottle last Saturday. *The place he saw the water pipit. It was upslope a little from the rebar. But which snow-covered lump is the rock I sat on?*

His mind went hazy. Everything looked the same.

How do I find a plastic bag somewhere under snow? Damn it! I should have gotten the book first.

He tugged the drawcord tighter on the jacket's hood.

Squinting into wind-driven snow, he scanned his monochrome surroundings.

What's that? Something stood out ... like it didn't belong. Beside a flat rock—one about the right size, he thought—teetered a plump, chicken-sized bird. It flicked snow from its brown and white-mottled back as it cocked its head and peered at him.

Garson gingerly stepped closer. Now only feet away, he heard it clucking softly between gusts of wind. *What's this bird doing here? All by itself? How weird!*

Maybe the bird thought the same thing of him. It blinked the snow from its eyes and scratched with a foot.

What? My bird book. It's standing on the book!

In an instant, it burst like a missile toward the glacier. As mysteriously as the bird appeared, it vanished.

With both hands, Garson clutched the book to his chest. An image flashed through his mind of his dad handing it to him. His trembling hands swept off the snow and tucked the book into his pack. *I'll look up the bird later, when I get to the trees.*

After brushing snow from his pants, he started the descent. Before him lay a bleak, white canvas, interrupted only by frosted lumps of rocks and boulders. Ragged clouds and swirling snow threatened to swallow the dull sweep of forest below. *At least the wind's at my back now.*

He focused on finding the Trust Rock. From that intermediate guidepost, he could hopefully navigate to the flagged forest path.

Footing on the snow-slicked rocks was super treacherous. Several close calls when a boot skidded out produced insane recoveries. *Slow down!* he scolded himself, remembering his accident last Saturday. With the worsening weather and little hope of getting help, he couldn't afford a fall.

By the time he spotted the Trust Rock, conditions were nearly whiteout. It was early afternoon. He hadn't eaten anything since a snack on the climb up the mountain. Hunkering against the downwind side of the Trust Rock, he gobbled a peanut butter and jelly sandwich and made himself drink nearly a quart of water. Dehydration lurked silent and deadly at high elevation. With the windchill now well below freezing, the water got Garson's attention. *Whoa! Brain freeze.*

Garson thought about calling his mom. With the storm blowing in, his mom would be extra worried. He thought about calling to tell her ... tell her what?

Yeah, mom, I'm fine, he'd say. Right!

He decided to wait.

How he wished he'd brought the GPS along. With it, he could walk right to the flagged forest waypoint. Instead, he pulled out the map and unfolded it on his pack. With the compass, he oriented it toward north the way Mr. Rock had shown him. *Cool. I just need to hike down the mountain's fall line, maybe ten degrees to the right.*

"I can do this," he mumbled, amid his doubts.

As the snow got deeper, the footing turned brutal. Step, step, step, slip, recover. *Place each foot. Go slowly,* he repeated. He felt like he was taking baby steps.

Ahead he saw the krumholtz drift, like a frosted green wave rising above an ocean of white. The forest lay not far beyond. He recognized the gray skeleton of a dead whitebark pine at the treeline. He'd make the tree his target.

As fast as it had struck, the storm relented. The wind died to a low roar and the sun gleamed through holes in the clouds, warming his face. A wave of relief swept through him. Now to attack the krumholtz barrier.

The tangle of branches was packed with snow. Pushing

through was exhausting, frustrating, and miserable. No matter what he tried—pumping his feet like a high-stepping drum major or pressing them straight ahead—his boots filled with snow. He gave up on scooping it out until he finally escaped the quagmire. That's when he felt his toes going numb. From knees to cuffs, his pants were sheathed in ice. He recalled images of gaiters and Gore-Tex pants in sporting goods catalogues. "Guaranteed to protect you from the elements," the ads read. *Note to self: gifts to request for Christmas.*

With the snow abating, the forest's edge sharpened, including a beckoning pink flag. Garson had scarcely enough energy for a jubilant "Yes!"

Once within the trees' protection, he chose a spot not far from where he called Mr. Rock a week ago. He plopped down beneath a sheltering fir. Its crown had intercepted the snow leaving a bed of needles beneath. His strength was sapped. The first shivers came on. He fumbled for and ate a handful of dried fruit. He forced down some icy water. It's times like this when the mind wanders to what you can't have. *Hot chocolate. Would that taste great! When I get home, I'm going to drink a huge mug.*

Reluctantly he dialed the cell phone of his mom's co-worker, Amanda. He worried his mom would detect shivering in his voice.

"Hi. This is Garson. Is my mom there?"

"Garson, where are you?" Lucy exclaimed. "Are you still on the mountain? There's a big storm coming in."

"Mom, it's okay. I'm alright," he reassured her while whacking shards of ice from his pants. "I'm on my way down."

The rest of the conversation went about the way he'd figured. She was frantic. He tried to make everything sound normal.

"I'll be at the trailhead in about two hours, maybe less. Will you call Mr. Rock?" Garson didn't want to talk to anyone else right now. "I want to save the phone's battery," he added.

After the phone call, there was one more thing to do. The bird book was a little soggy, but intact. Thumbing open the cover, a hand-written inscription to Garson from his dad read, "Birds fly because they believe they can."

He could almost hear his dad's voice saying the words.

Garson flipped the pages to the section with grouse and quail. Ptarmigan. It looked right, and ptarmigan were the only chicken-like birds who lived in the alpine. Of the three species listed, only one lived here. *It had to be a white-tailed ptarmigan I saw.*

Ptarmigan lived up here all year long, he read, *just like Buddy does. How do they do that?* A shiver wracked his spine. *And it's still not winter yet!*

Snowflakes filtered into the forest gaps. It was getting colder. *Sitting here ain't gonna help.*

Through the trees, brush, and deadfall, Garson wound his way. Sheltered by the trees, the game trail was mostly snow-free. Deep in thought, he barely noticed passing flag after pink flag.

His mind summoned Buddy's image, his hand on her face, and what she told him.

He thought about the birds. *I left the book when I was watching the pipit. But then the ptarmigan helped me find it. Weird.*

Next the owl flashed before him, the one he'd mysteriously seen in the forest. *Maybe I can tell Kira. Maybe she'd be interested in what they're planning to do to the forest.*

Images and ideas flitted inside his head like birds in an aviary. Trapped yet bent on freedom. *Maybe these strange things all fit together.*

Down the game trail, past the lake, and after the last mile, a familiar sight greeted him … standing beside his gray pickup truck was his teacher. Both were relieved and overjoyed to see each other.

In less than an hour, Mr. Rock dropped him at the house. His mom was waiting.

There was a lot to tell her, but first, "Will you make me a cup of hot chocolate?"

"I'll make us both one. Extra marshmallows?"

After Garson left her, Buddy followed the edge of the ice. She searched, not certain where Oreo would be. *Is she still on the glacier?*

Through the swirling snow and mist, she spotted and ran to her. After some lavish nuzzling from Oreo, Buddy said, "You climbed onto the glacier. I'm happy you could."

"You saw me above you?"

"Sure did. Your shoulder must be better, even if I didn't see you war-dancing."

"Much better," Oreo laughed. "Let's shelter behind these boulders. Before you tell me what you learned, I'll tell you this. I was worried at first, I almost ran down the glacier to protect you. But I was laughing too hard."

"Why?"

"Seeing you with those two. You looked out of place—the only one who had four legs and wasn't black!"

"Baha, ha, ha," Buddy laughed so hard it showered snow from her coat.

Oreo's expression turned thoughtful. "I've lived a long life.

I've seen and survived wicked storms, thundering avalanches, and a bear attack," she said with a glance to her shoulder.

Shaking her head slightly from side to side, she said, "But in the last three months, I've seen more unusual things than any goat probably has."

"What do you mean?"

"Being led to a starving three-day-old kid by a raven. Watching her play and talk with a marmot who named her Buddy. And now, you're talking with a man—a boy—as your raven looks on. Sometimes watching you is ... like a dream."

"When it's happening, it all seems natural to me. Like, why wouldn't I war-dance with a belly-sliding marmot named Maurice? Then afterward, I sometimes don't understand it."

"I don't understand either until I look back. Then I see everything happened for a reason. You were chosen to be the goat-Keeper of the Legend for a purpose. You have special gifts, not the least is your vision of the future. What makes me especially proud is the way you use those gifts to help others."

Buddy's very deepest feeling, the one she'd been holding back, burst forth, "I couldn't have done any of it without you, Mom."

Oreo straightened her neck. Her eyes filled with love. "That word ... 'mom' ... is the best thing you could ever say to me."

As they nuzzled, wind and snow assailed them. But they were mountain goats. To them, snow and cold were not a foe. Their ancestors had persevered through far worse.

The future, however, might script a different story, but not because of *wintry* weather.

Chapter 24
Runaway Hand

Sunday to Thursday, September 22–26

Sunday morning broke like December, not late September. Drawing his bedroom window curtain, a winter wonderland greeted Garson. Eight inches of snow had blanketed Pinewood overnight. *What's it like where Buddy is?*

He looked at his watch—eight o'clock. After yesterday's adventure, he'd slept like the dead. But he awoke fully energized.

"Hey sleepyhead, I guess the smell of pancakes and eggs woke you up," Mrs. Strangewalker said as Garson charged downstairs from his bedroom."

"Hope there's plenty."

In between mouthfuls, Garson rehashed yesterday's events. "It was super amazing! I was really talking to Buddy. Who knew anyone could really do that ... talk with an animal?"

"Like in a Disney movie," his mom said.

"Only it was real."

Garson gushed more details. Only a pause to refill her coffee cup interrupted his mom's attention.

"I started to see what it's like being a mountain goat, and the troubles they might have. I mean, if it keeps getting warmer ..."

Garson paused, deep in thought. A clump of snow tumbling from a Ponderosa pine outside the window caught his mom's attention. "It's so pretty outside today," she said. "I think I'll find my winter boots and go for a walk. Want to join me? We can talk more then."

Garson hesitated. Another time, he might have said yes. But not today. His mind was racing. "I want to start writing up my science fair project. Before I forget some stuff I'm thinking about."

She raised her eyebrows. *This is my son? This boy who wants to do schoolwork on a Sunday, rather than go outside? What's the world coming to?*

"Okay. But you're going to miss your chance."

"What chance?" Garson said, while dabbing syrup and egg yolk from his plate with a chunk of pancake.

"To beat me in a snowball fight," she quipped, showing her schoolgirl smile.

"Really tempting," he grinned, "but I want to get started on this."

"You know what I think?"

"What?"

"I think glaciers and mountain goats have changed you into a studious student."

Garson gave her his scrunched-mouth, lips-twisted-to-one-side look, the one he reserved for when he was deep in thought or irked. "You mean a nerd."

"I think more like a junior scientist. Hey, I'm proud of you. I'll clean up here. You get started on what's going to be a terrific science project," she beamed.

"Thanks."

Garson began writing about what was happening to the world's glaciers—the project's introduction. Then on to what he did at Shining Mountain Glacier. He wrote in ink on a lined yellow pad. He wrote, not in complete sentences, but however the ideas stormed him.

After filling the first page, he couldn't make his pen keep up with his brain. Writing had always been drudgery. Not now. A peculiar and unexpected feeling overcame him. For the first time in a long time, maybe ever, he wanted to be best at something. He wanted to create the best science fair project. And he understood why he wanted to do it.

He feared the interruption of booting up his computer and word processor might freeze his brain. Instead, he kept scratching pen on paper. Zooming from one sentence fragment to the next.

When he stopped, an hour had elapsed. "Amazing," he said aloud. *I've never written an assignment this fast.*

Of course, to Garson, this had become far more than a school assignment.

Mrs. Strangewalker was a stickler about TV. She felt an hour, maybe two, of TV in the evening was enough—even on weekends. That included an hour of news, including the channel where she worked, of course. Wednesday was a weekly exception for *Nature* and *Nova* programming that aired on PBS. Odd how a TV producer would allow such limited TV time, but she prioritized time for Garson's homework, outdoor activity, and reading.

Reading? Really? Almost as much as speaking in class, Garson hated reading! At least until he began his science project. Now, after dinner most days, he would vanish into his room.

When Wednesday came, however, Garson didn't miss watching *Nature*. This week's program called the Amazon Rain Forest "the lungs of the Earth."

"That's how important the rainforest is," the narrator said. "The forest cleanses the air and slows the planet's warming by capturing carbon dioxide. Much of it is stored in their trunks."

When the program ended, Garson bolted to his room. His thoughts streamed like searchlights illuminating one object after another in the dark. Following an hour of Googling, and another hour of writing, his head had emptied, like an upturned vessel. It was time, he realized, to read what he'd scrawled over the past four days.

Two things struck him. First, what he wrote was a mess. It needed lots of "fine-tuning." Second, he'd written about way more than his science project, mostly prompted by what Buddy told him. *If I learned all that from Buddy in an hour, what could people learn from other kinds of animals, if we could talk to them?*

Mountain goats, ravens, rosy finches, water pipits, and ptarmigans all lived up there on Shining Mountain. Most people never saw them; knew little about them. How will—how is—climate change affecting them? And what about the plants and insects? An image materialized of Roark spearing a butterfly. *With Roark's appetite, there need to be lots of insects.* Garson grinned. *Stop it! I've gotta focus on the glacier.*

But his gut told him it wasn't going to be easy. Not anymore.

That week at school, Garson kept a low profile—even lower than normal. He went to classes. He tried to pay attention. His mind kept straying to the glacier, Buddy, Roark, the ptarmigan. He itched to get home each day and resume his research on the computer. Work on his writing. At school, only science class—that mysterious and absorbing study of nature—held his attention for a full fifty minutes.

When English class ended Thursday morning, Garson lingered.

"Do you have a question, Garson?" Mrs. Cullen asked as she organized papers on her desk.

"I was sorta wondering."

"Yes?" she looked up.

"The assignment you gave us yesterday, the essay we have to write ... Well, I'm doing a project for the science fair, for Mr. Rock's class. Can I use that for my essay?"

"Which type of essay would it be? Descriptive? Narrative? Argumentative? Maybe expository?"

"I'm ... I'm not sure." he began to wish he hadn't asked.

"Nor am I. A science fair project isn't written in essay form, is it?"

"Probably not. I guess it's more the scientific method form."

"Very good," she raised her eyebrows, as Garson looked at the floor and probed his pocket for the jackknife prohibited inside school.

"You know what's an even better reason?"

Garson shook his head, wanting to disappear.

"You'd be trying to escape your English assignment. I know from your time in class, English probably isn't your favorite subject. But I've had plenty of students who felt like you. And you know what?"

Hearing the change in her voice—less critical, more caring—he looked up. "No."

"Many began to like writing, once they found something they wanted to write about," she smiled. "Tell me about your science project."

"It's about how glaciers are melting. How climate change is causing it."

"Maybe you've found something to write about. If you adapt it. Write it as an essay."

Garson sensed she knew how Shining Mountain captivated him.

"Tell you what. I'll look over your written science project if you like. Just to check on grammar and how it reads."

Garson broke into a huge grin, "Would you?"

"Yes, after you've polished it as best you can. When's it due?"

"We've gotta have our projects done the week of Thanksgiving. Then Mr. Rock wants us to talk about them in class," both his voice and eyes lowered.

"Have you started?"

"I've been working on it this week."

"That's great. Best to get writing assignments done early. Give them time to ferment a little, then revisit and revise before they're due."

"Mr. Rock said something like that."

"A very good teacher he is. For the essay, decide what most interests you about glaciers. Once you know, I'm guessing the story will come to you. Then craft it to read like an article in a magazine. All right?"

"Yeah," Garson said, feeling both relieved and energized. "Thanks for talking to me about it."

With a bounce in his step, Garson spun toward the door. Before reaching it, he turned back, "Mrs. Cullen."

"What is it?"

"I know the essay's not due until the end of October. But if I get stuck when I'm writing, can I ask you for help?"

She smiled widely, amplifying the creases beside her eyes, "Yes. I'll look forward to reading it."

Chapter 25
Full Disclosure

Friday to Saturday, September 27–28

As Wednesday became Thursday and Thursday became Friday, Garson grew increasingly antsy. *When are the slides of the glacier going to get here?*

He avoided bugging Mr. Rock. His teacher would tell him when they arrived.

When science class ended Friday, Mr. Rock motioned Garson to wait. "Your slides are here. They came in yesterday's mail."

Garson's face lit up. "Did you look at them?"

For the last two weeks, he worried his roll of Ektachrome images might be poorly exposed. Or worse, entirely blank.

"Yup. Spread them across my slide viewing table last night." He paused, waiting to see if Garson was going to take a breath. "You did well. They came out great."

Garson gushed, "Cool. When can I see them?"

"Tell you what. I said I'd take care of having the prints made. After I pick them up, you can come by my house. We'll compare the two sets."

"That'd be great! Thanks."

Mr. Rock followed the other students and Garson out the classroom door and locked it. Garson watched him disappear down the hall, the tan rucksack slung over one shoulder.

Beyond his teacher, he spotted Kira talking with two other girls. He thought about waving. His hands stayed stuck in his pockets.

Behind him, Garson heard a ruckus down the hall. "Leave me alone!"

Billy and Todd were teasing another sixth grader who was new to their school this year. Her name was Koko Tail Feathers. She was dark-complected and quiet in class, like Garson. She wore a beaded Indian bracelet and tie in her gleaming black hair.

"Tail Feathers? I don't see any feathers back there," Billy guffawed.

"Maybe they're tucked inside," Todd chimed in, followed by his donkey laugh.

"Leave me alone, I said!"

Billy reached for her shoulder to spin her around. Koko pushed his arm away.

"I only wanna have a look," Billy sneered.

Whenever they taunted him, Garson felt self-conscious, vulnerable, peeved. But seeing this provoked a deep anger inside. *I can't just stand here and watch.*

When Garson reached them, his face felt hot. "Didn't you hear her? Leave her alone."

"Well look whose gonna play hero, the Straaaange Walker," Billy said.

Garson didn't care what they might do to him. The bullying had to stop. Now.

Other students began watching from both ends of the hall.

When Billy's hands shot forward, Garson ducked, but not enough. As he tottered backward, he felt a hot spot where a fingernail had scratched his cheek.

"Take that, little man," Billy barked.

Undeterred, Garson started back at him as an unfamiliar voice behind Billy boomed, "Hey, I saw that!"

"Owww," Billy cried, as his right ear got twisted in a vice grip.

Billy Cribbs was big for a sixth-grader. Robert Tail Feathers was bigger, the biggest eighth-grader in his class. Nobody called him Tail Feathers, which was odd because Robert cherished his surname and heritage. "I'm Blackfoot proud," he would say. He played running back on the football team like a battering ram. It earned him the nickname Tank.

No one gave Robert Tail Feathers any lip.

With hair pulled back in a ponytail and his ebony eyes shining fiercely, he said in a low voice, "What do you have to say to her?"

"I didn't do anything," Billy squealed as Robert torqued his ear.

"Nothing? You think I can't see?"

"Let me go."

"You. Grab his other ear," he said to Todd, who looked like a scared puppy about to pee himself.

"Grab it or you're next."

Todd grimaced and gingerly pinched Billy's left ear.

"Now pull." As Robert pulled one ear and glared at Mr. donkey-laugh, Todd cringed and tugged the other. Billy's face turned beet red. "Stop, stop. You're hurting me. What d'ya want me to say?"

"Apologize," Robert answered.

"Okay, okay, I apologize."

"For what?" Robert tugged harder.

"Owww! For teasing her."

"Gonna do it again?"

"No. I promise. Just let go."

When Robert released his ear, Billy hissed, "You too, jerk!"

Todd let go and slinked away.

"Now get lost," Robert said. "And don't give *him* any more trouble either," motioning toward Garson.

After the creep crew beat feet ahead of Robert, and the onlooking students shuffled and muttered toward the cafeteria, Koko said, "Why did you do that?"

"You mean try to make them stop?"

"You *know* how mean those bullies are."

"Yeah. I try to ignore them. My mom always says if I retaliate, it'll make things worse."

"So why did you now?"

"Because ..."

"You think I can't stand up for myself. Like I need my brother or you to rescue me," she said indignantly.

"No."

"Then why?"

"Because ... they did it because they think you're different, like me."

"You mean because of our last names?"

"Well, yeah," Garson paused. "And because you're Native American, right?"

"What of it?"

"I didn't mean it that way. I just think because you are, it makes it worse how they treated you." Garson wanted to avoid her eyes.

She looked at him intently. There was something about him she hadn't seen before, from her seat across the classroom. And because she hadn't talked to him.

"What about you?"

"My dad's Shoshone. Nobody else knows," Garson confessed.

"I'm Blackfoot. Our tribes were enemies," her eyes outshined her gleaming smile.

"I guess."

"See you later. Oh, and thanks."

Garson hadn't noticed Kira had been observing from a distance.

"You're bleeding," she said as she walked up to him.

Garson wiped his cheek with the back of his hand and saw the blood.

"Are you okay?"

"Yeah. You saw what happened?" he asked, hoping she hadn't. He felt stupid and deflated because his efforts had failed. And that Koko's brother had to save his bacon.

"Most of it. Enough to see you were the only one who tried to help her," she smiled.

There was something about her. Every time they talked, he felt funny inside, like after eating super spicy food.

"Hey, have you got a science fair project yet?" Garson blurted, surprising himself.

"I thought about a couple of things, but haven't decided," she shook her head, making her hair shimmer in the light streaming through a window. "Why?"

"I saw something last week I'd like to show you. Maybe you could use it."

"What is it?"

"It would be easier to show you. It's in the woods where I live."

Kira furrowed her forehead. "In the woods?"

"Yeah. It's along the trail where I run. Do you like to run, or hike?"

"Sure. Tina and I run sometimes after school."

"Well, if you're not doing anything tomorrow, maybe we could go then." He didn't want time to think this over and get cold feet.

"I don't know," she said, wondering what this was all about.

"Really, I think it's important, what I want to show you. And maybe a good project."

Kira agreed. She'd meet Garson at his house next morning, that is, if her parents didn't object.

Chapter 26
Not So Simple

Saturday morning, Kira's mother drove her to Garson's. She visited with Lucy and Garson until she felt she wasn't delivering her only daughter to some wackos on the edge of town.

"I'll pick you up in a couple of hours," she said before driving off.

Yesterday at dinner, when Garson told his mom that a friend was coming in the morning to go running with him, Mrs. Strangewalker was both surprised and curious.

"Oh? Who is it?"

"Her name's Kira."

You don't say?

Now, as she watched them melt into the trees, she was not only surprised and curious but pleased. *This boy who's had no close friends has asked a seventh-grade girl to go for a run with him. That's nearly as shocking as his talking mountain goat!*

For early fall, September twenty-eighth felt more like summer, warm enough for tee shirts and shorts. Puffy white clouds drifted lazily above the Ponderosa pines and the mountains beyond. Cottonwood and aspen leaves were turning golden. It was perfect.

From the house, they intercepted the trail paralleling the foot of the mountains. Familiar ground to Garson. As they jogged, they talked about school, friends (well, Kira did), and about the woods. "This is very cool to have this right by your house. I mostly run on the roads where I live, or at the park. But it's pretty small."

Her eyes, lively and green as spring leaves, darted left, right, and up to the forest's soaring canopy.

Garson named the birds they saw, and some they only heard. "Chickadee. Stellar's jay. Cassin's finch. There goes a robin."

"I knew *that*, Mr. Audubon," she snapped, reprising his cap.

"Sorry."

"Oh, I'll forgive you, just this once." She pointed to her right, "What's that one I hear now?"

"The one going 'yank, yank, yank'?"

"Yeah."

"White-breasted nuthatch."

"Oh."

After half an hour, Garson stopped. "This is where we leave the trail."

"Why?"

"It's up there. What I want to show you."

Garson wove effortlessly through the trees and shrubs. Hesitantly at first, Kira followed.

When he reached the place the owl had led him, he said, "This is it. What I wanted to show you."

For several minutes he filled her in on what he'd learned by calling the local US Forest Service Office. *For someone quiet as a mouse in school, he's sure talkative out here,* Kira thought.

"Some of these trees have probably been here longer than Pinewood has been a town."

She tilted her head and frowned, "How would you know?"

"Well, look at that big Ponderosa pine." Garson walked to it and rubbed its rusty orange bark. "See this black scar on its trunk?"

"Probably from a fire. So?"

"Small trees don't survive forest fires. They get burned up. But old ones grow thicker and thicker bark. It protects them."

"So?"

"I did some research after I found this spot last week. There hasn't been a forest fire here in a hundred years."

"You mean this tree was big enough then to survive the last fire?"

"Yeah."

Garson concluded, "The Forest Service person told me they plan to auction these trees off. Sell them to the highest bidder."

He led her to the sign that read, "Cutting Unit Boundary."

"They want to cut down all these painted big trees? For what?"

"Best I can tell, make them into lumber."

Kira scanned the forest in disbelief. "They can't," she shouted.

Garson could hear the same anger in her voice that he felt.

"How'd you find this place, anyway?"

He told her about the owl, observing if her expression betrayed that she thought he was crazy, or just really weird. Her face only looked thoughtful.

Garson turned and started making the strangest sound, Kira thought, "Wheeeooo. Wheeeooo."

From a distance floated similar flute-like notes.

Garson called again, "Wheeeooo."

A gray, robin-sized bird drifted from the forest and landed in a nearby tree, "Wheeeooo."

To Kira's amazement when Garson called once more, it flew to a tree limb not ten feet away!

"How'd you do that?"

Garson shrugged.

"Do you know what it is?"

"A gray jay. Pretty cool bird, huh?"

As he checked out the jay, she studied this wiry boy with cryptic brown eyes. She said, "I heard you talking to that girl on Monday, the one Billy and Todd were hassling."

Garson suddenly felt uneasy.

"I heard you ask her if she was a Native American. Then I heard you say your dad was too. Is that true?"

He faced her and tried to read her eyes but couldn't. "Yeah. He's Shoshone. From Wyoming."

"Maybe that explains it."

"Explains what?" he replied more emphatically than he wished.

"Why you know so much about trees and animals, like this jay, or the owl you followed here. It's like you can speak with them."

You don't know the half of it.

"Maybe it's in your DNA."

"What?"

"It's what's in your blood. Why you care about the outdoors and nature more than other people."

Garson sometimes had such thoughts. But never did he talk about them, not even with his mom. Yet somehow, he felt comfortable with this volcano girl. Like maybe ... just maybe, they could be friends.

"Okay, this is terrible what they want to do to the trees. But Monday, when you asked me to come here, you said it could be a science project. What? Like I'm going to keep this from happening for science fair?"

Garson described the *Nature* show about the Amazon he watched. And what more he learned on the internet about forests capturing CO2 during photosynthesis. "I was thinking it might be a neat project to measure how much CO2 these trees take up. And then show what would be lost if they were all cut down."

"Then why don't *you* do it?" she challenged.

"I already have a project."

"Convenient," she shook her head in frustration, "Do you have any idea how hard this would be? Measuring how much carbon dioxide this forest uses, or just *this* one tree," she pointed to the closest pink-painted fir.

"I know. But I think it's important."

"Agreed, Mr. climate guy. Doesn't mean it would be easy to do. It's a project for a scientist, not a science fair."

"Mr. Rock could help you. At least you could talk to him and see if he thinks you could do it."

"Why me?"

"Well, you don't have a project yet. And I asked because I think you're really smart. If anyone could do it, you could."

She frowned at Garson, then looked at the trees. Their crowns were swaying in the morning breeze—breathing. *They don't get a say in this. Nobody asks them if they want to be two-by-fours.*

She shook her head sideways, "This isn't like comparing water samples from different ponds. Or building a volcano." As she sighed, Garson saw the faintest of smiles. "I must be crazy. Okay, I'll talk to Mr. Rock about it."

"Hey, this project could win first place!"

"Or end in failure and wreck my science class grade."

As they left the cutting block, Kira asked, "Do you talk other people into doing stuff like this?"

"I think just you."

They jogged to the trail, and then back toward Garson's house. Both were deep in thought when Kira said, "Race you to your house."

Could he have caught her? Probably. Instead, he watched her

arms pumping and her red hair streaming behind her. *She runs like a gazelle.*

Mr. Rock thought Kira's idea was terrific, but complicated. After some discussion, he made suggestions about researching how such a study could be done. Two days later, after seventh-grade science—the last class of the day—they spoke again.

"Yes, this will be challenging. And out of my wheelhouse." He scratched the back of his head. "But I know a botanist at the college. If she has time, perhaps she could get you started. I'll let Professor Woodson know you'll call her. Still interested?"

By now Kira was wishing she hadn't gone on the run to Painted Treeland with Garson. "I guess so."

She called the number Mr. Rock gave her. Dr. Anna Woodson said she'd meet with Kira, listen to her idea, and then see if there was a way to design a project like this for seventh-grade science fair.

Normally outgoing and chatty, Kira nervously reeled off her idea, as she understood it, about carbon dioxide uptake through photosynthesis in the forest and how the trees keep the carbon from returning to the atmosphere.

"Whoa, whoa, whoa! Trying to do all that would be heroic, but way above a seventh-grade science project," Dr. Woodson responded. "Maybe a college graduate degree."

I knew it. Garson got me into something that's impossible.

"Here's what might be feasible. Instead of trying to estimate how much CO2 the forest absorbs and sequesters over time, let's keep it simple. You might be able to estimate how much carbon is stored right now in the painted trees at your study site."

At the whiteboard, Dr. Woodson diagramed the calculations necessary. She spewed terms like forest stand basal area, allometric equations, and conversion factors in a steady stream. Kira's head was spinning. *That's keeping it simple?*

Kira was unresponsive. To Dr. Woodson, she looked dazed.

"But don't worry, it's something you could do without measuring everything yourself, that is, if the Forest Service has completed their inventory and timber appraisal. If so, they can tell you how much wood is in those trees. Then I'll help you convert pounds of wood to pounds of carbon stored in them."

Kira appeared to regain consciousness.

"It would be a very worthwhile project. And you strike me as a very capable student."

The compliment did wonders for Kira's outlook.

"Did you say there is more than one species of tree marked to be cut?"

"Two. Ponderosa pine and Douglas fir." Something she remembered Garson telling her.

"Perfect. There's the basis for a hypothesis, right?"

Kira blinked and scrunched her forehead, straining to formulate a response. "I think it would be to compare the two species."

"And what would you compare?"

"The carbon in one species compared to the other."

"Good. Now can you state it as a hypothesis?"

"Umm." Kira's eyes pinched nearly shut, recalling her lessons on the scientific method. "I would hypothesize there's no difference in the amount of carbon stored in Ponderosa pine and Douglas fir trees."

"For which ones?"

"For all the painted ones they plan to cut down."

"Perfect. There's your hypothesis. Now your job is to see if it's true or false."

Simple, except, Kira didn't know how many trees in Painted Treeland were painted. And certainly not how many of each species. *I sure don't want to have to count them.*

Bigger problem, Dr. Woodson said she'd need to know the trees' biomass, the scientific term for how much they weighed. *No way I can figure that out!* Her project completely depended on if the Forest Service could tell her those things.

I hope they know. If not, I'm toast.

Chapter 27

Legendary Secret

September 30–October 2

Garson got to science class early Monday, hoping to avoid Billy and Todd in the hallways. Mr. Rock shot Garson a grin, "I should have the prints on Wednesday. If you want, we could look them over that evening, maybe after you've had dinner. Otherwise, it'll have to wait til Saturday."

"I'll ask my mom about Wednesday. Can I let you know tomorrow?"

"That'll be fine. Of course, she's invited too."

At dinner, Mrs. Strangewalker said Garson could go on Wednesday. "But I don't want you riding your bike in the dark."

"It won't be dark after dinner."

"How about when you're done looking at the photos with Mr. Rock?"

Garson gave her his scrunched-mouth, lips-twisted-to-one-side look.

"I'll drive you. When you're done, call and I'll pick you up." Garson didn't mind at all when his mom said she wouldn't stay.

Mr. Rock lived on the east side of town, the side opposite

Garson's. Built of tan and rusty brownstone, fitted block upon block, the one-story house looked fitting for a geologist, Garson thought. A cedar shake roof had collected drifts of needles from two towering Ponderosa pines. Beneath them, Mr. Rock was splitting wood with an ax when the Subaru pulled up.

After exchanging a few words with him, Garson's mother drove away.

"Well, come inside Garson," Mr. Rock said, wiping perspiration from his forehead with a bandana.

A heavy wood door opened into the living room. Facing a large fireplace, built of the same rock as the house, two overstuffed chairs framed a leather couch. The fireplace wall was paneled in barnwood streaked in blacks, browns, and rich burnt orange, like the old barn along the road to Shining Mountain. Garson followed his teacher down a hall and through a doorway.

"My office," he announced.

A well-worn oak desk and leather-covered chair, which looked still older than the desk, ruled one wall.

On the desk were twin computer monitors. Big ones, with two four-drawer, oak filing cabinets beside the desk.

But Garson's eyes were quickly drawn to what adorned the walls and a long table along the wall opposite the desk. On the table were collectibles, not the kind from gift shops—what Garson called junkerias—but hand-made items of wood, leather, and soapstone. Each begged to be held. Front and center was a two-foot-long spike.

"Is this a walrus tusk?"

"Sure is, from the Bering Sea."

"Can I pick it up?"

Doc Rock scooped it up and handed it to Garson's outstretched hands. It was heavier than he expected. Garson rubbed his fingers over the polished ivory surface. *This was once a tooth in a living animal.* One that weighed a ton or more.

"It's something you don't see much outside a museum," Mr. Rock said. "Most folks wouldn't want somebody else's tooth in their house." His eyes twinkled as they had that Saturday in August. The day he and Garson first met to talk about the Shining Mountain Glacier.

Garson admired the tusk, running his thumbnail along the longitudinal cracks in the enamel. "This is so cool," he murmured.

"I bought it years ago in a Yupik village. Back when it was still legal," he added.

Garson lowered it as gently as an egg to the table. He gazed at the collection of framed photos arranged on the office's beige walls. Many were mountain scenes with snow and ice in abundance, often with people dressed like Eskimos wearing heavy boots and gloves and carrying climbing ropes, ice axes, and bulging backpacks.

He stepped close to a large map framed behind glass, titled "Glaciers of the Cascade Range." Speckled across the topography were hundreds of white polygons, each labeled in ice-blue print. The biggest were in far northern Washington state—Mount Baker, Mount Shuksan, and others in and near North Cascades National Park. The southernmost was Lathrop Glacier—two skinny lobes clinging to the north face of Mount Thielson in southern Oregon.

Next Garson fixed onto a 11 x 14 photo framed in gray barnwood. Behind a dozen people posing on the deck of a boat was a massive wall of vertical ice. The ice disappeared into a foreground of inky water. The photo was snapped as a huge block of ice crashed into the sea.

"Is this you?" he pointed to one of the parka-clad people.

"In Glacier Bay, Alaska. A bunch of us attending a conference in Juneau got a close-up look at a calving glacier. Quite a sight!" he quipped. "Most of those tidewater glaciers are receding. Some have retreated almost fifty miles since explorer Joseph Whidbey first saw the bay and its ice in the late 1700s.

Fifty miles! Really? Garson marveled. He could have listened to this man for hours. "You've seen a lot of neat stuff doing your work."

"And lots of changes," he nodded.

Of all the images on the wall, two captured Garson's attention most. The first was a small black and white photo above the desk. Doc and a woman. *Maybe his wife?* Garson took notice; no children were in any pictures. His mother's voice echoed in his head, "Don't ask personal questions when they're not invited."

In the other photo, a young lanky man in shorts and a t-shirt stood grinning in front of a glacier. The camera slung over his shoulder was a Nikkormat. Garson knew that camera and that grin. "This is you?"

"Yours truly. And you know the glacier."

"Shining Mountain?" Garson's head snapped around and saw his teacher's toothy smile.

"It's when I took the pictures you've now retaken yourself." His brow furrowed slightly as he brushed the thinning hair from his forehead. "Time we got to looking at both sets, side-by-side."

On the desk were two stacks of 8x10 prints. Mr. Rock's and Garson's. Ten in each stack. Of the three bracketed photos Garson took at each reference point, Mr. Rock had chosen the best exposure to print. Starting with reference point number one, they compared the prints. His teacher pointed out how the glacier's leading edge had receded on every photo pair. He also noted subtle changes in the ice over the four decades separating the pairs.

When they finished, Garson exclaimed, "Wow, I knew there were differences when I took the pictures, compared to the photocopies you gave me. But this is way more impressive, seeing them side by side."

"Sure is. Photographs don't lie. The glacier has shrunk this much in a mere blink of an eye."

They leafed back through them once more. "There won't be space on your poster for all ten pairs. I'd suggest you pick three."

Garson did and laid the three pairs side by side. His eyes were drawn to the foreground of the images.

They both fell silent until Mr. Rock prodded Garson, "What other changes do you see?"

More than the glacier and the pint-sized plants pushing up through cracks of the newly exposed rock, something in the foreground captivated Garson. Something fantastical. Something he knew to be true. *The newly exposed rock—all of it—was limestone.*

In his mind, he was back there with Buddy. Learning the mountain's truth. Recalling the questions which flooded his head. Questions that seemed to paralyze him, as if not knowing how to proceed in the dark of night.

Reaching out, he touched the photo on his teacher's desk. The one he'd taken at reference marker #1. He heard his breathing, felt his heart beating.

"Mr. Rock, can I ask you a question?"

"Of course."

"When you were on Shining Mountain, did you see anything

unusual?"

"Like what?"

"Something you couldn't explain with science, like it was beyond geology."

He studied the boy's deep-set eyes, "Why do you ask?"

"Because the last time I was there, I learned something about the mountain. Something I wouldn't know if I hadn't been told."

"Told?"

"Yes. And I've been wondering if you know there's something unusual up there too?"

The teacher furrowed his brow. He'd been troubled for forty years by what he'd seen, or rather, hadn't seen. He'd kept it to himself. No one in his profession would believe him. Worse yet, he'd be dismissed as a crackpot if he shared it.

"There's something there ... It's something contrary to everything I know about glacial geology. Then after the slides arrived and I looked at your photos ... well, that's when the mountain's mystery really hit me."

He ran his fingers through his hair and shook his head. "But first, what is this about someone telling you about the mountain?"

Garson felt nervous, uncertain, but relieved all at the same time. *I can trust Mr. Rock. He'll understand.*

"It's about the rock by the glacier." Garson pointed to the limestone on his photo. "It's out of place on top of all the granite."

"You recognized that yourself?" he asked, astounded at Garson's insight.

"No. I didn't get it. But when I went back the second time, she showed me and explained it."

"She? Who's she? Who did you run into up there?" Doc blurted, unable to suppress his astonishment.

Garson hesitated, then launched into his amazing encounter with Buddy at the glacier. As strange as the mountain was, why would a talking mountain goat seem any stranger?

Garson wondered if Mr. Rock was okay. His eyes never left Garson's as he unwound the tale. But he didn't speak a word. Finally, Mr. Rock pinched his eyes shut, opened them, and slowly nodded his head up and down. "That's what struck me about your photos. All that limestone rimming the glacier is ... nowhere else high in the mountain chain do we see that. Only in the valley. It truly defies explanation!"

Despite his remarks, Mr. Rock's face betrayed inner doubt. He was struggling to process what Garson told him. *Does the boy really mean he talked to a mountain goat? He surely seems convinced of it. I'll just leave that be for now.*

He broke into that toothy smile and exclaimed, "Of course, it's tough to top a talking mountain goat. Especially one who can teach geology!"

Garson ignored the humor in the statement. "Please don't tell anyone else about her. Only my mom knows, and now you."

"That'll be our secret, just the three of us," he smiled and added, "and the mystery of how all that limestone found its way up the mountain."

"I know. I see myself there all the time, looking at it with Buddy. But you haven't been back to the glacier in forty years, right?"

"Exactly."

"So, what was it? If you couldn't see the limestone cuz it was covered by ice, what troubled *you* about the mountain back then?"

"That's seventh-grade geography. As glaciers advance downslope, the ice bulldozes a border of earth and rock along their leading edge. Moraines. On Shining Mountain there's no moraine. No sign of one at all. But you already know that."

Garson thought about his treks up and down the mountain: the forest, the krumholtz belt, the alpine meadow, then the glacier with its skirt of limestone. "I didn't really think about it. Yeah, there's no ridge of rocks and boulders like in all the other pictures I looked at of glaciers. Why not?"

"Like the patterned limestone, I think the lack of moraine can only suggest one thing." He paused for a sip of cold coffee with Garson hanging on his words. "Shining Mountain, and the glacier now covering its summit, are not a result of textbook geological processes."

He could barely believe he spoke the words. In all his years visiting glaciers around the world, only Shining Mountain was like this. One of a kind.

Garson balanced on the edge of his chair.

"Moraines form as glaciers rapidly grow during cold, snowy periods. Shining Mountain's glacier must have formed late in the Pleistocene, a time when the continent's glaciers were just holding their own. Then it began to retreat. As glaciers melt and shrink, they expose land they once covered."

"You mean right after Shining Mountain's glacier formed, it began to melt?"

"Probably not right away, but within a few hundred years. The real question—and the biggest mystery—is this. How was the mountain created? The limestone we can see in your photos may well go much higher, possibly to the summit. We can't know," he shook his head, and pinched his eyes shut.

"I think I know," Garson all but whispered. He told Mr. Rock what Buddy had briefly told him. The mountain had been built. "I don't know who built it. She didn't say. But it was so the mountain goats could escape what she called the Great Warming. For a better place to live. A place that was higher and colder."

Mr. Rock's eyes were wide open now, fixed on the photos. *Of course, not only is the limestone out of place, it looks like the slabs were positioned!*

"I believe you. I believe you talked to a mountain goat. And you learned the mountain was somehow built thousands, not millions of years ago. And then the glacier formed. It's a better explanation than anything I can come up with."

Garson could almost see the lines on his teacher's face deepen as he talked.

"Of course, it doesn't make me feel any less troubled that such a thing could happen."

He raised his eyebrows, smiled, and laid one hand on Garson's shoulder, "I'll tell you something more. One reason I never mentioned it to anyone is my fondness for Shining Mountain. I didn't want the place invaded by scientists, the media, and curiosity seekers because of something I said. Without any road or trail access, the mountain and its glacier have received scant attention. That's kept its landscape pristine. And its solitude. Things becoming all too rare anymore. I guess I feel protective cuz I want to keep it that way. Heck, few people even know there are mountain goats living up there!"

Garson thought about his teacher's words. *Maybe that's why Buddy helped me when I was stuck. She didn't know to be afraid of people.* But he knew there was more. Buddy took a chance. She, too, was seeking help—for her band. Now, Garson silently renewed his pledge to aid her.

After he called his mom, they stepped outside. The air felt like fall had arrived.

"You've been busy, with more than this project and your other studies."

Garson looked questioningly at him. "What d'ya mean?"

"Kira's project. She told me how she chose it. Melting glaciers and the other harm from carbon dioxide emissions are one side of the equation. Kira's project looks at how forests help regulate carbon. How the planet is continually healing itself, finding balance. Both are important. I'm really pleased you're taking a larger view and helping another student."

In his gut, his teacher's words reminded him of what he deeply missed—his dad's devotion and encouragement. Not that his mom didn't provide it. It was just different.

Mr. Rock's house sat far enough east that the tiptop of Shining Mountain was visible above the forested slopes. A waxing three-quarter moon and millions of stars stippling an inky sky illuminated the glacier. It looked to Garson like a shimmering flying saucer. Indeed, it held secrets as alien. *Up there,* he mused, *is a small mountain goat who knows things that humans do not.*

He felt the mountain pulling at his core. Drawing first his eyes, then his heart, then all of him to its summit. *Mr. Rock is right. It's special. And its legend needs to be protected too.*

Chapter 28

Departure

Tuesday, October 1 (10 days after the big snow)

The day before Garson visited Mr. Rock, fall's fickleness struck Shining Mountain. It was cold, not for mountain goats, but for the hoary marmots and golden-mantled ground squirrels who had long since entered their winter dens. Cold for the rosy finches and American pipits who had migrated south. And cold for dormant plants which would wait a full seven months before their lives renewed in spring. Each species abandoned life on Shining Mountain, not strictly because of cold and snow, but for lack of food they could neither find nor make themselves.

Early storms—like the one ten days ago when Garson learned about the rocks at the glacier—were mere previews of coming attractions. Over a foot of white had covered Oreo and Buddy that night. Afterward, Buddy wasn't excited to see winter's main event.

The next morning, she had cried, "How will we ever get to Goat Mountain now? I can hardly move."

"We'll get there. In a few days, this will melt away."

Buddy's frown and doubtful look prompted Oreo to add, "You'll see."

"But what will we eat until then?" Buddy lamented, bucking chest-deep snow.

"That's what we've got feet for," Oreo said. She rose and pawed a wide depression in which she exposed dried grasses. Buddy quickly joined her in the feeding crater.

With the hollow in her stomach filling, Buddy asked, "Do you think Garson got caught in the snow? He only has two legs, not four like us."

With no idea if a boy would get trapped in snow, Oreo tried to ease Buddy's fears. "He left before much snow fell. He's probably fine."

Buddy felt reassured, as she often did by Oreo's words.

As Oreo expected, mild weather returned to Shining Mountain. The dump of snow ten days before had melted. By comparison, a couple of inches overnight felt like kid's play. Buddy rose and shook. A shower of crystals sparkled in the morning light.

She hopped into a war dance, prancing and tossing her head. The sight ignited Oreo. The two romped and scattered snow as if they'd feasted on locoweed. As suddenly as their frolic began, Oreo stopped as if embarrassed by her clowning. Some nuzzling and licking of faces reinforced their bond and love for each other.

"Will it snow again, like the day Garson was here?"

"I thought you liked snow?" Oreo jested.

"On the snowfield below Goat Mountain, where our band snow-lounges. But not everywhere!"

"We don't get to pick and choose," Oreo said while Buddy wrinkled her forehead with displeasure. "One thing we do get to choose is when we leave for Goat Mountain."

Buddy's expression changed to pure excitement. "When?"

"I don't sense an approaching storm. We'll leave tomorrow."

Buddy hop-skipped, then turned serious. "I want to talk to Mystic or Tenanmouw before we leave Shining Mountain."

"That's only proper. We will before we go."

Before dawn, they rose for an early feeding. It was a glorious morning to begin their journey home. In August their journey had taken two full days. Buddy was now five weeks older. Five weeks stronger. With Oreo's shoulder healed, they hoped to travel swifter.

Searching for Tenanmouw on the north side of the mountain would take them farther from Goat Mountain. Instead, they contoured south not far below the glacier.

"When Tenanmouw led me to the goat cliffs, I saw some of their band there. I hope we don't have to go as far to find Mystic."

"There's no telling where she might be. You know better than me how big this mountain is."

With her belly full, Oreo resisted the urge to stop and ruminate the morning's meal. They were in a hurry.

An eagle glided overhead. Buddy crouched. Memories of last June's close calls shook her. Even though she'd grown from house cat size to thirty pounds, her two-inch horns did little more than amuse the eagle. No problem. Oreo was there to defend her with twin nine-inch daggers.

"Everything in good time," Oreo reminded her whenever Buddy became impatient about not being bigger. She could hardly wait to grow full size, or at least as big as Elbuort, the yearling whose favorite pastime was bullying her. Because she and Oreo would reunite with their band soon, Elbuort was creeping into her mind. *Maybe he's changed,* Buddy hoped. *Ha! Not likely.*

Where the mountain's western slope fell away toward the cliffs, they spotted them. Several white figures looked up from their grazing near the glacier's margin. The smallest, a kid, bounded toward her.

"You're Buddy. Remember me? I'm Snowdrift," she said and romped excitedly.

"She knows you," Oreo said, wondering how she did.

"We met when I first got to Shining Mountain. Before you got here."

Buddy and Snowdrift play-chased, feigning head butts and tossing heads from side to side.

Soon the others, all older goats, trotted their way. As they neared, a look from her mother brought Snowdrift to her side.

"I wondered if you were still here," the biggest nanny said. "Only Tenanmouw has seen you since you arrived."

Buddy and Oreo instantly recognized the nanny. Setting her apart from the others was her blind eye. Cold and gray as granite, it had made Buddy shudder when she first met the Shining Mountain band's matriarch. Seeing Buddy recoil, Mystic had said, "I still have one good eye to see what's standing right before me. And to envision the future."

Being wise was necessary to become a trusted leader. An old matriarch like Mystic, or Spirit of the Goat Mountain band, had survived ice-slicked slopes, avalanches, predators, and challenges from subordinates vying to be in charge.

"We came to find you. Because my shoulder's healed, we're returning to our band on Goat Mountain."

"As you should. A band needs its matriarch."

Oreo could read between the lines. Mystic didn't regret their leaving.

Oblivious to Mystic's not-so-hidden message, Buddy said, "But we hope to return after the winter's snows are gone."

Only Snowdrift seemed to take any pleasure in Buddy's words.

"I welcomed you to our mountain while your shoulder healed. But whatever kinship you share with Tenanmouw does not entitle you to bring your band here."

Oreo tensed. She felt the ridge of hair on her back spring up. Living her whole life on Goat Mountain, she'd only known goats from her band. She felt ill-prepared to handle this challenge from Mystic.

"Our home no longer provides for us as it once did. Buddy's the only kid who survived this year."

"And because my home is better, you think that you can move here?"

Looking to Oreo for guidance, then back at Mystic's seeing eye, Buddy said meekly, "It's what the Legend tells us to do."

"Legend or not, each band has its own home. We have enough resources for ourselves. For how long, I don't know. Make do with what you have," Mystic insisted.

Buddy felt hurt and confused. *Was I wrong to believe the Legend was telling me to find a new home?*

"It's time we go," Oreo nudged her. "Better we leave than to risk trouble."

Retreating off Shining Mountain, Oreo had never seen Buddy look as defeated. She resisted Buddy's pleading to find Tenanmouw. "Let's see what he has to say."

Oreo knew it wouldn't matter. The matriarch's word would be final. In goat society, it had always been so.

As they reached the belt of krumholtz, a raven called above them, "Toc, toc."

Buddy's mood ticked up. *I think that's Roark. Maybe he can help.*

The raven tucked his wings and plunged. Effortlessly, and

not a moment too soon, his wings unfolded to break his fall. Light as a feather, he lit upon a block of granite.

Buddy trotted up.

"I see you're returning to Goat Mountain," said Roark.

Buddy detected tension in his voice. "Is something wrong?"

Uncharacteristically, Roark ignored a passing moth. "I fear there is."

Oreo joined Buddy, "What did he say?"

"It's Battenmouw. Roark says he's not well," Buddy's voice trembled. "Ever since Roark told me that Battenmouw agreed, I haven't felt like I'm *really* the goat-Keeper of the Legend. To be sure, I need to hear it from him. But what if before we get home, Battenmouw ..."

Oreo felt the anguish in Buddy's voice. This brave kid had achieved so much, and yet doubts persisted. Not unlike Buddy, Oreo's untested position as matriarch left her anxious. *Do the others know that Spirit passed the mantle to me? And will they accept me as their leader with our future uncertain?*

Deep down, she knew such self-doubt was pointless and destructive. Especially for a nanny of her age and wisdom. Regardless, they each had much to resolve on Goat Mountain.

"First, we need to get home. Then we'll find Battenmouw," Oreo said with all the assurance she could summon.

Still, something more plagued Oreo. The boy Buddy met at the glacier. *Was Buddy right to trust him? Were his intentions to help us sincere? Or might he be no different from men in the wasteland? Even if by accident, might he further imperil our band, and the Shining Mountain band as well?*

Chapter 29

Triumph and Treachery

On Friday, the last week of October, everyone in English class—well maybe not everyone—was eager to get their essays back. Near the end of class, Mrs. Cullen announced, "This and the final exam will make up the largest part of your grade."

Garson's heart skipped. *I think I did a good job. I sure hope so.* His hopes were as much to win her approval as to get a good grade.

Up and down the rows she went, handing students their essays. Yes, she still graded written prose the old-fashioned way. Garson guessed, that like his mom, Mrs. Cullen also preferred to read books with paper covers rather than ones on electronic devices. He did too.

Her smile was broad when she handed Garson his essay. Written on top was a red "A" and the words, "Great work!"

Garson thought he might explode. *An "A" in English? Me?*

As students filed out at the end of class, she called him to her desk.

"Thanks, Mrs. Cullen," he blurted.

"You proved when you apply yourself, you can write well. You earned that grade."

Garson saw a twinkle in her eye, like Mr. Rock got when he told stories about climbing up glaciers. "I think you can do even better," she added.

From her desk drawer, she pulled a magazine, *NatGeo Kids*. She opened to a full-page announcement for a writing contest. One for kids only.

Whoa! National Geographic!

"Me?"

"Yes. I think you can write a competitive essay."

Garson felt such a mix of excitement and nausea.

"With the timely subject you've written about here, and by weaving in more of your experiences at the glacier ... well ... it's worth a try. But the writing must be excellent. You'll have to work hard at this."

It didn't take him long to decide. When he got home, he showed his mom the essay with the red "A" on top. "And there's this writing contest Mrs. Cullen thinks I should enter. The winners get published in *NatGeo Kids*."

"Garson, that's wonderful! You're going to do it, aren't you?"

"Yeah. Mrs. Cullen said she'd be my sponsor."

Garson was more excited than he let on. *This is how I can help Buddy. Not write about only the glacier melting, but how the warming is affecting life up there. How can people not want to change what they're doing to the environment when they learn this?*

Garson felt stressed to get his science fair project done. He was sure he'd run out of time. Then, when he finished, it seemed like forever until next week—the week of Thanksgiving. Way too much time to stress about next Monday's oral presentation. He felt nervy. His mom could tell. Mr. Rock could tell. He was eager to show his classmates what he'd done. *But why do I have to talk? And in front of everybody?* At night, his dreams about talking to his class always ended in disaster, with the creep crew heckling him or the sudden onset of lockjaw. *At least I have my tables of data and photographs to tell the story.*

That morning his mom drove him to school. Along with the others, he placed his trifold poster in Mr. Rock's classroom. There were more students in sixth-grade science than could present in one fifty-minute period. Mr. Rock arranged with the faculty for his eleven o'clock class to resume after the noon lunch hour. The previous Friday, Garson had learned more about the presentations. They'd be in alphabetical order. Ugggh! He'd be sweating it out all morning until the afternoon.

The first student, Amy Anderson, opened her poster on Mr. Rock's desk. She introduced her project, and explained its purpose, methods, findings, and conclusions. Amy didn't seem one bit nervous. Garson felt envious.

One by one, as Mr. Rock called their names, each student marched to the front of the room, opened their trifold poster on his desk, and gave their talk.

Billy Cribbs was third. "My project is metamorphosis in frogs."

With his usual swagger, Billy described the three stages of tadpole development, pointing to crude, hand-drawn figures on the poster.

Garson heard the student sitting behind him whisper, "That must have taken him days to make."

Mr. Rock allowed time for a question after each presentation. Amy asked Billy, "Why didn't you include an adult frog?"

Billy answered with typical sarcasm, "Cuz it's not a stage of metamorphosis."

The room was silent for a moment until Mr. Rock corrected him, "Indeed, the adult form is the final stage of the frog's metamorphosis. Wouldn't you agree?"

Billy's ruddy complexion turned redder. "I s'pose."

"Garson you raised your hand when Amy did. Do you have a quick question?"

Garson could tell others were also enjoying watching Billy squirm. He couldn't resist asking the obvious question, "Shouldn't you include the egg as the beginning stage?"

That made Billy's face tighten, "No."

In the interest of time, and out of pity, Mr. Rock thanked Billy for his presentation and called the next student. Billy glared at Garson while storming back to his desk.

When the bell sounded at the end of class, only four of fifteen students were left to present. Garson would be first, followed by Koko Tail Feathers, Sue Thompson, and Todd Ulander. As students filed out of the room, Garson was glad that Billy didn't follow him to pull some sick prank. Over his shoulder, he saw him huddling with Todd near the posters.

Ever since the incident when Robert Tail Feathers torqued his ears, Billy had been seething. His ears still hurt a day later. Worse yet, he felt humiliated and vulnerable, something every bully detests. He made Todd swear he'd never do anything like that again—the way he helped Robert stretch his ears. Or else!

Billy vowed he'd get even. Not with Robert, but with Garson. "But we've gotta be clever," he told Todd. No telling if Robert might show up again to rescue that loser, Strangewalker.

In the weeks leading up to the day of science fair class, Billy hatched his plan. Their plan. Todd would be a full partner ... or else! Todd didn't dare say no.

To avoid giving away what they were plotting, they were careful. So careful they only let a couple of snide "Straaaanges" slip from their lips when passing Garson. No more "Call Me Stupid" signs stuck to the back of Garson's jacket. No more accidental-on-purpose tripping in the hall.

All was going as planned.

Chapter 30

Science Fair

As his classmates drifted from the cafeteria back to Mr. Rock's room, Garson avoided eye contact with Billy. He knew the question about the frog egg had infuriated him. He could feel Billy's beady eyes bore like daggers into him.

Mr. Winkleman, the math teacher, took a seat at the back of the class once again. Mr. Rock had asked him to help judge the student projects. The two of them would decide which two students—the top ten percent—would move on to regional science fair competition.

When everyone was seated, Mr. Rock said, "Garson, you're next."

With his heart thumping in his ears, Garson walked to the front of the room, collected his poster, and placed it on the desk.

"My project describes the melting of glaciers. To do it, I studied the Shining Mountain Glacier this summer."

When he opened the poster, his jaw dropped. Where three pairs of photos should have been, comparing what he photographed to what Mr. Rock had photographed forty years before, there was white space! The captions remained, but *no photos*. His head swirled trying to make sense of it. His palms were sweating before his talk, now he thought they might start dripping. Billy and Todd were sniggering. A couple more students joined in. Garson looked to Mr. Rock for help.

"Quiet everyone," he scolded, looking straight at Billy and Todd. "Does anyone know who removed Garson's photos?"

Silence.

"Garson, do you want to continue without all the elements of your poster?" He paused and added, "Or you can give your presentation after the Thanksgiving break at the beginning of class next Monday."

Garson squeaked out, "Next Monday, if that's alright."

"That's fine. Of course, this means the judging of student projects will be delayed until then. Now let's finish with the final presentations, and there had better not be any surprises like the one we just saw."

It was as stern a voice as his class had ever heard from their teacher. You could've heard a pin drop as Koko stepped to the front of the room.

In her quiet voice, she explained how she'd compared traditional Blackfeet medicine to drugstore-bought topical ointments to relieve muscle pain.

"A very interesting project, Koko," Mr. Rock said. No one asked questions.

Lastly came Todd Ulander. Todd was not an unlikable kid unless he was around Billy Cribbs, which he usually was. Billy seemed to get Todd to do whatever he wanted. "Maybe Billy makes him feel good," Garson's mother had said. "The ones who hang with bullies are usually as insecure as the bullies are."

Todd introduced his project, "Comparing water samples in Black Bear Creek."

The creek flowed through Pinewood. Todd had collected water samples from above and below town. He sent them to the state water quality lab for testing.

"The water is better above town. It has lower coliform

bacteria counts. Those kinds of bacteria can make you sick. They're getting into the creek from Pinewood."

"You say the water is better," Mr. Rock said, "but on your chart, it barely meets state standards for people to drink. Why do you think the bacteria counts aren't lower?"

Todd fidgeted. "I don't know."

"Maybe because people camp up there in the forest? And how could we determine their effect on the water?" Mr. Rock asked the class.

No one answered, though Garson wanted to.

"Let me ask this another way. How could we determine if the water above town, where Todd sampled, could be even cleaner? With lower bacterial counts."

Garson tentatively raised his hand.

"Yes, Garson. What do you think?"

"You could sample much farther upstream or maybe, better yet, collect water from Cub Creek."

"Why there, anyone?" the teacher asked.

"I know," Todd said. "Because there aren't any roads or buildings and other stuff that might pollute Cub Creek."

Garson smiled to himself. *Just what I would've said.*

"Very good Todd. By also sampling water from Cub Creek your project would have a control—meaning a location without human influence. You'll remember we talked about controls back in week three when I covered setting up scientific experiments."

Todd beamed. His expression quickly changed when he saw Billy glaring at him.

Garson's mom was furious when she learned what had

happened. "It's those two bullies again, isn't it?"

"I don't know who did it. Please, Mom, don't talk to the principal about this." Garson knew he had to find a way to deal with it on his own.

Before the following Monday, Mr. Rock had new prints made to replace the missing six. After placing them in his poster display, Garson still felt anxious. He still had to do his talk on Monday. Just him. And among those in the room would be the culprit who took his photos. That would be on his mind while he tried to concentrate on what he was saying. Tried not to look as nervous as he felt. Tried not to sound lame. He could hardly wait for Tuesday.

Because science class wasn't until eleven o'clock, Garson asked Mr. Rock to lock his poster in the classroom closet for the morning. Safeguard it with microscopes and other valuable stuff. No problem.

Eleven o'clock rolled around and Garson's stomach was doing flip-flops. Although he'd done it about a dozen times on Sunday, he couldn't stop rehearsing it in his head. Mr. Rock laid Garson's folded poster on his desk. *I guess I'm ready*, Garson thought. Everyone's eyes felt trained on him. He wished the Swiss Army knife was in his pocket.

To everyone's surprise, Mr. Rock started class with an announcement. "Garson is the last to present his science project. We all know what happened last Monday when it was his turn. Well, I know who took Garson's photographs. I'll deal with that after class."

It was all Garson could do to keep his head from twisting to see his classmates' faces—especially a certain one.

"Okay, Garson."

As he rose and walked up front, Mrs. Cullen entered the room. She took a seat next to Mr. Winkleman. Garson was elated. Seeing her there somehow made him feel less nervous.

"My project's title is 'Shining Mountain Glacier, Then and Now.'"

He gave his talk as if on autopilot. As smoothly as in his bedroom yesterday. He tried to observe the rules of public speaking: look at everyone in your audience, try not to look at the poster except to point things out. Speak clearly. Don't rush!

Each time his eyes found Mrs. Cullen, her smile calmed him. When his eyes landed on Billy Cribbs, the kid looked red-faced and antsy. Like he'd rather be on another planet.

"The edge of the glacier has retreated ninety-five feet. That's a lot in forty years. My conclusion is the melting of the glacier is most likely because of increasing average annual temperature." Garson pointed to the upward trending line on his temperature graph. "Scientists have found this for glaciers on every continent."

Pointing to his previously missing photographs, "These pictures from then and now show the difference in the glacier."

As his classmates applauded, he realized his hands weren't sweating.

"Any questions for Garson?" Mr. Rock asked.

Not a hand went up.

"Well, I have one. If you wanted to know more about what's happening to Shining Mountain Glacier, what would it be? And how would you research it?"

Garson and Mr. Rock had not discussed this. No problem. All his reading had prepared him for such questions. He knew what glaciologists were studying.

"I'd want to know how much ice the glacier is losing. I'd want to measure the area of ice lost using satellite imaging from different years."

"Is that all?"

"Well, the glacier is probably shrinking in thickness. I'd want to know that too."

"Very good. Anyone else?"

"Very well, I'll post the two top projects for sixth and for seventh grades on the bulletin board in the hallway. Check at the end of classes tomorrow."

In the remaining time, Mr. Rock introduced the next block of study. When the bell rang and students filed out, he motioned Billy Cribbs and Todd Ulander to his desk. To Garson, Billy's face looked drained of color, like he'd seen a zombie.

Mr. Rock accompanied them to the hall where Mr. Humphner, the school principal, was waiting at Billy's locker. "Let's have a look inside Mr. Cribbs."

Billy and Todd knew their goose was cooked.

As Mr. Humphner and Mr. Rock marched the thieves to the principal's office, Billy asked, "Will this affect my chance of making the top ten percent?"

Mr. Rock quipped, "No. Your project didn't have a chance without this stunt."

"I never should have gone along with this," Todd groaned.

But how did the teacher and principal know?

Over the holiday weekend, Kira had called Garson.

"I know who did it. Who took your project photos on Monday," she said with a steely voice.

"You do?"

"It was those two jerks, Billy and Todd. I was passing by the science room during break. They were laughing. Then Billy took some papers from his pack and put them in his locker. Bet you anything it was your photos."

"Did they see you?"

"Nope. I was in sleuth mode. One of my superior talents. Besides, they were too busy yukking it up to notice."

"Wow. I wonder if I should tell Mr. Rock?"

"Already done."

The theft went down like this. When Monday morning's science class ended, Mr. Rock stepped out of the room to speak with one of the students. During those few minutes he was in the hallway, Billy and Todd opened Garson's poster and, you guessed it, they swiped the photographs. Billy stuffed them in his daypack before Mr. Rock returned to the room. The heist was complete.

Sure enough. Billy was dumb enough to have left the photos in his locker ... for a week!

On Tuesday after classes ended, sixth and seventh graders gathered at the science bulletin board. Mr. Rock was posting the competitions' winners. Garson wiggled forward through the crowd, close to Kira. They both let out a whoop! Their projects each made the top ten percent in their classes.

On Wednesday, the winners' names were among the morning announcements. Instead of the school secretary, Mr. Humphner himself congratulated the winners over the intercom.

Even bigger, for the Wednesday evening local news, a TV crew showed up at school. Lucy Strangewalker not only produced the segment, but she also interviewed the students and their teacher, Mr. Rock. Garson was stoked. Lots of people would hear about his project. But you'd have thought his mom won the lottery. Next evening Kira and her mom joined Lucy and Garson. They celebrated with pizza and cokes.

Chapter 31
Partnership

Garson had a secret. One he didn't share with anyone at school ... not even Kira. He didn't share it with his sorta best friend. *If I did, who knows what Toby would think?*

Only his mom and Mr. Rock knew. He'd had to tell each of them.

A day didn't pass without him thinking about Buddy. Over and over. Her parting words stuck like super glue, "We want to know, will you stop the warming?" He vowed to keep his promise to her, though stopping the planet from overheating was a tall order for a twelve-year-old boy.

Garson had another secret. One he'd kept even from his mom ... especially from her. Okay, he had to tell a few people because they were invited. Saturday was his mother's birthday. He vowed to do more this year than merely wish her a happy birthday. She'd trusted him to go to the glacier. Twice. She even believed he had talked to a mountain goat. That deserved something special ... a surprise party!

He invited her friend Amanda and two other co-workers to come, plus Mr. Rock, and Kira and her mom.

Only one problem. He had to hope she wouldn't have to work on Saturday. Seemed like her part-time job had become full-time lately. What he needed was a plan, a pretext so that the guest of honor wouldn't miss her party.

So, Garson asked her to go hiking with him Saturday afternoon. Maybe back to Lupine Lake if snow didn't block the road. Before they would leave for the trailhead, the others would arrive at the house.

Garson was new to party planning. He didn't have specifics in mind. Because Kira's mother offered to bring the cake, that big item was taken care of. Cool! He'd only have to wait for everyone to show up and shout, "Surprise!" Oh, and he'd make iced tea. That he knew how to do.

When he got home from school on Friday, his mom was sitting on the couch. Something wasn't right. She didn't look up. It was as if she was asleep, or in a trance. But she wasn't.

She was just staring at her lap. In it, she was holding a framed picture. He couldn't see the image but recognized the frame. Softly he said, "Mom, are you okay."

"No, honey, not really."

Garson sat beside her. Now he could see the picture of his dad.

"What's happened, Mom?"

She sobbed deeply, almost convulsively. In a hoarse voice, she said, "The Marine officer who came here, the one who told us your dad was missing in action? He called me at work."

Garson felt his entire body tighten. Despite the years, details of the captain's uniform and face flooded back. He waited, fearful of what she was about to say.

"He said they had learned your dad was imprisoned with other Marines and soldiers."

Garson's face was filled with electric anticipation.

"How do they know?"

"He couldn't give me details. National security, I guess. He only said the building where they were being held was being surveilled. I suppose with drones or satellites, but he didn't say."

In his pocket, he squeezed the jackknife so tightly his hand hurt.

She paused and looked squarely at Garson. "He told me some of them escaped."

"So, Dad's alive?"

Garson searched her eyes for confirmation.

"They don't know for certain."

Garson's dread turned to excitement.

"The Marine officer said their captors killed several, but not all of them. They recovered their bodies. They know their names." A big gasp wracked her. "Dad wasn't one of those."

Garson leaped from the couch and spun wildly across the floor, repeating, "Dad's coming home! He's coming home!" One part of her wanted to join Garson. Jump for joy. But a stronger, darker part held her back. The part that doubted. The part that wanted to protect her son, and herself, from more disappointment.

All these years, she'd tried to find out about John through the Red Cross, Iraq and Afghanistan Veterans of America, and other service organizations. A slew of disappointing calls with Captain Anderson yielded nothing, although she knew it was no one's fault. They didn't know. It seemed as if he'd vanished from the earth, which is how other families of MIAs she talked with so often felt.

For five years, I didn't know he was alive. Then this call today.

Garson halted in front of her. "He is, right? Dad's alive. He's coming home."

"They think so. I think they know more than they told me.

But he told me this was a positive turn. They plan to rescue the survivors … if they can."

"When?"

"He didn't say, honey." She lowered her eyes.

Garson didn't know what more to ask. This news was like the dreams he used to have. The kind he hadn't had for a long while.

They sat together, quietly looking at the photograph. Lucy had several of John, but this one she kept on her nightstand. It was the last picture she had taken of him. She took it at Camp LeJeune Marine Corps base days before he deployed to Afghanistan. Standing beside his Ford pickup, one arm propped on the hood, his broad smile with teeth gleaming whiter than white contrasted with tanned skin and jet-black hair. He looked happy, despite what awaited him in Asia.

"When will they tell you more?"

"I'm not sure," she squeezed his hand. "Until now, I didn't even know he'd been captured … that he was alive."

She smiled. "I want to believe he's coming home too. But we shouldn't get our hopes up too high."

While his mom fixed dinner, Garson retreated to his room. His feelings were all jumbled. He threw himself on his bed, wishing, yet not daring to believe he might see his dad again. Years of pain and anger he'd kept bottled inside, bubbled up. He pounded the bed and sobbed.

Then the emotion seemed to dry up like raindrops on hot pavement. He sat up, reached into his pocket, and retrieved the knife. He rolled it over and over in his hand, picturing his dad giving it to him.

"You're old enough. This might come in handy one day," he'd said.

Garson laid it on the bed. From his bookshelf, he pulled the bird field guide. Before placing the book next to the knife, he read his dad's words on the inside cover. Words he'd read a hundred times before. "Birds fly because they believe they can."

From the back of his desk drawer, he removed the single photo he kept there. Garson and his father on the North Carolina beach. His father smiled for the camera while seven-year-old Garson grinned up at his dad. On the back of the photo, he read his dad's words, "Semper fi—always faithful, Dad."

Garson looked at these precious possessions for a time. Cherished memories and haunting thoughts ricocheted through his head. His heart was pounding. *He's gotta be alive.*

Then he turned away.

If his dad came home, what would he want to show him? How could he recreate the last five years? *Start with what's most important.*

Garson went to his computer. He printed out the report for his science fair project. He printed the article he wrote for the *NatGeo Kids* competition. He slid both into a big mailer envelope. Next, he pulled up a photo he'd taken on his mom's phone and uploaded to his computer. One he'd shown to no one else. His pulse quickened as the printer spit out the 8 ½ x 11 image. Buddy and Roark at the Shining Mountain Glacier.

He wanted to see her again. Two things stopped him. The chance of snowstorms on the mountain now that it was fall. And she might not be there. Buddy had said she'd be leaving soon for Goat Mountain. And then there was a final problem. He'd have to convince his mom to let him hike to the glacier again.

Each time he looked at her image, which he did every day, his mind replayed their meeting. The photo helped him remember each detail of that amazing experience. The image kept her alive, like having an invisible friend. Except Buddy was *real.* And there was something more. It was like ... well, like he and Buddy— and maybe even Roark—had a partnership. One dedicated to tackling the threats to their home. In their own way, Mr. Rock and Kira and Mrs. Cullen were part of it. They just didn't know it.

And, of course, his mom had supported it all. She had trusted him. She made his changed life possible. A birthday party was the least he could do to thank her.

He slipped the photo of Buddy and Roark into the envelope with the other things. He'd give it to his dad when he returned. *He'll come back,* he assured himself. *He has to. Then mom and I will tell him all about what's happened since I started this science project.*

Lost in these thoughts, a huge smile creased his face.

Toward the spicy aroma of spaghetti sauce cooking, he padded downstairs. When she saw him, Lucy smiled at her grinning son. "One meatball or two?"

"How about three?"

Throughout dinner, they spoke little. Yet their smiles remained.

Chapter 32
Trust

As noon approached the next day, Garson's anticipation mounted. When his mom wasn't looking, he'd peek out the front window.

Mr. Rock arrived first. As Garson had asked, he parked and waited for the others far enough down the street to avoid being obvious. When they knocked at the door, Garson was there to open it. He held a finger to his lips.

"Who's there?" Lucy called from the kitchen.

"Come see."

"Happy birthday," they shouted in unison when she saw them.

"Garson, you planned this?"

"Sure did," he grinned ear to ear.

Kira placed the chocolate cake on the dining room table. It joined a pitcher of iced tea.

"So, this is why there are two pitchers of iced tea in the fridge. You don't know how hard it was not to ask you about that," Lucy said.

After hugs were shared and Lucy was handed a fistful of cards, the celebration began. Besides a rousing chorus of Happy Birthday and opening of cards, there was much else to celebrate. Both Garson and Kira would be competing in the science fair regionals.

"After not making regionals last year, I'm proud of you, Kira, for upping your game this year," Mr. Rock said.

Kira cast Garson a sly glance. "I think it all depends on the project you pick. Carbon sequestration in forests is a step up from an exploding paper mache volcano."

As the laughter subsided, Kira's mother focused on Garson and her daughter. "What I think is great about you two is how much work you both put in. And how your projects dovetailed."

"That's right," Mr. Rock said. "You both managed to address climate change in very different though complementary ways. Working together, even if on different projects, is an important aspect of doing science. I'm proud of you for suggesting Kira's project to her," he said to Garson.

"Not as proud as I am," Lucy followed.

"I really think the segment on the local news you did was first-rate, Lucy," Kira's mother said. "It was a fine tribute to the work these two put in, and to the school's science program."

"Thank you. Well, I'm just going to clear the table while everyone visits."

"I'll do that."

"It's okay, Garson. It'll only take me a few minutes."

As Lucy began stacking plates and silverware, Mr. Rock rose and gathered those on his side of the table. He followed her into the kitchen.

Since everyone arrived, Lucy hadn't stopped smiling. It felt good sharing conversation and laughter with these wonderful people. Once away from the others, however, her thoughts returned to her husband's plight. Her hands shook, tumbling silverware into the sink.

"Are you okay, Lucy?" Doc said, seeing the worry on her face.

"Oh, I've just got some things on my mind," not realizing that he had followed her to the kitchen.

"If it's not too forward of me, I want you to know what a fine job you've done with Garson. I mean, you've given him exactly what he needed."

"Oh? How so?"

"You trusted him to make his own decisions, including his own mistakes."

"You mean like letting him wander into the wilderness alone?"

"Yes, and to make friends with a mountain goat," he quipped as they shared a hearty laugh.

"Can I ask you something?"

"Of course."

"Before this year, Garson had such a hard time. School was a struggle. He didn't care about it. Not even sports, like running, which he's so good at. In fact, there wasn't much he cared about doing, especially with others. He was kind of a lone wolf, I guess. You played a large part in bringing him out of his shell. May I ask why you took Garson under your wing?"

"I saw something special in him. I'm not saying he's any smarter than other kids. It's his curiosity and his motivation to pursue learning on his own. And, well, I know he's had some problems to deal with. Troubles with other kids, and his father being gone. I know what it feels like, missing someone you love."

At once, he saw a change in Lucy's expression. Her face tensed. She grabbed the counter.

"What is it?"

"Oh, I've had a rough 24 hours."

She was quiet for a bit, but the sincerity in his face told her she could trust him. "I heard from the Marine Corps yesterday. They believe John is alive. Escaped from a Taliban prison."

Unaware of her husband's plight, Doc was stunned.

"It's the first time in so long I've let myself think I might see him again." She dried her hands on a towel, cleared her throat, and said with a smile, "I should get back to the others."

After everyone left and quiet replaced the laughter in their home, Garson said "I want to show you something."

Lucy followed him up to his room. Arranged on his bed she saw the knife, the book, the picture of him and his dad. To those treasures, Garson had added a barnwood-framed picture he'd taken of his mom. He'd taken it on their hike to Lupine Lake then moved the file to his computer from her phone. In the portrait, she was smiling brightly with a bunch of purple daisies clutched to her chest.

"It took me a while to get it framed."

She held it close, feeling the emotion rise. Since hearing about John yesterday, everything seemed to make her want to cry. Whether out of anticipation or fear, she wasn't sure.

"I love it. Thank you, honey." She hugged him.

He took the photo from her hand. He placed it next to the one of him and his dad. "Soon we'll all be together, I hope."

She realized that was what she felt. Sublime hope. Something she'd not felt for so long.

She hugged him again. "You just reminded me of one of my favorite sayings."

"What's that?"

"Where there's a possibility, there's hope."

"Do you think Dad will be home for Christmas?"

"I don't know. But if not, I hope he'll be here to see you at the regional science fair. He'll be so proud of you. Hey, what's in that big envelope?"

He handed it to her. Looking at the science fair report and the article he sent to *NatGeo Kids*, she felt a rush of pride and happiness. Then she pulled out the last item. The photo of a mountain goat kid and a raven perched near it.

"Is this her? Is this Buddy?"

Eyes locked on the photo, he grinned and nodded.

"You must have erased this from my phone. Why didn't you want me to see this before?"

"I dunno."

"I think you do."

Garson fidgeted. "When I met her and could talk to her, it was so amazing. I didn't want anything to spoil it. I wanted to keep it just for myself, even this picture of her."

"But you'd already told me about her."

"I had to, so you'd let me go back to the glacier to see her again." His expression relaxed, "But I learned something."

"What?"

"I learned it's okay to trust others and share something special. I learned it because of how you and Buddy trusted me."

Lucy thought her heart might melt.

Far, far above Pinewood, a kid mountain goat, nurtured by her adoptive mother and guided by a wizardly raven, sought to fulfill her destiny. As the most recent keeper of an ancient legend, she trusted its prophecy. Now Buddy was homeward-bound to join her band. She would try, with Oreo's help, to convince them to leave the only home they'd ever known.

In Pinewood, a twelve-year-old boy pursued his own challenge, supported by his mom and mentored by a benevolent science teacher. Garson had vowed he'd find a way to stem the crisis in Buddy's lofty home. Because of a magical encounter with a kid mountain goat, his school science project had become much more.

These two kids' lives had unexpectedly intersected. What lay ahead would test their determination and their improbable bond.

The Science Behind Legend Keepers

Geology

There are three groups of rocks: igneous, sedimentary, and metamorphic. In this book's story, Shining Mountain is made of granite, a type of igneous rock whose origin is molten magma. But Garson learns from Buddy that the top of the mountain is made of limestone. Limestone's a type of sedimentary rock, often found at lower elevations where sediments have settled. Under pressure, they've compressed into stone. When Mr. Rock was on Shining Mountain 40 years earlier, he didn't see the limestone. Why? Because it was covered by the glacier. That alone tells us that the glacier had melted and retreated a lot in just four decades. And in real life, this is happening to glaciers all around the world. With global warming, we could say that glaciers are now an endangered species—that is if they were a living thing, which is how Garson thinks of them. To learn about geology, start with *Geology for Kids: A Junior Scientist's Guide to Rocks, Minerals, and the Earth Beneath Our Feet* by Meghan Vestal or *Super Earth Encyclopedia* from DK Children.

Global Warming

Global warming, also known as climate change, is the long-term warming trend of our planet's climate. In the past, the Earth has been warmer than today, and sometimes much colder. But it's the speed at which Earth is now heating up that's so alarming. Since the Industrial Revolution, the burning of fossil fuels has accelerated. Their combustion releases carbon dioxide and other heat-trapping gases that accumulate in our atmosphere. This is intensifying what's called Earth's greenhouse effect. For the first time in history, humans, not nature, are the main cause of Earth's warming and changing climate.

Modern societies have not previously experienced the consequences of such climate warming. In Yellowstone National Park, for example, temperatures are likely the warmest they've been in 800,000 years. Melting of the planet's polar ice and mountain glaciers is acidifying oceans and raising sea levels. Scientists also believe that more severe weather events, including both heavy rains and severe drought, will increasingly cause hardship for human populations. On top of habitat destruction, pollution, and human exploitation of plants and animals, climate change is now a leading threat to life on Earth. Thousands of plant and animal species are threatened with extinction. Some won't be able to adapt fast enough to survive. This is certainly true in the planet's polar regions and high mountain ranges which are warming fastest.

Many books, websites, and magazine articles advise how humans can make a difference by adjusting our behavior and lifestyles. One place to start is the book *A Kid's Guide to Global Warming* by Glenn Murphy.

Pleistocene Epoch

Also known as the Great Ice Age, this 2.6-million-years-long geological time-period ended about 12,000 years ago. During the Pleistocene, massive ice sheets covered much of the northern hemisphere of our planet, including Canada and southward into the northern United States. At the close of the Pleistocene, a warming climate was responsible for the melting of most of the ice, leaving behind isolated glaciers in Alaska, and scattered high mountain areas of western Canada, Washington, Montana, Wyoming, Oregon, and California. The ice sheets and remnant glaciers gouged canyons and carved impressive peaks we see in these mountains today.

Glaciers

Glaciers are masses of ice, sometimes hundreds of feet thick, that move slowly downhill (or rather down mountain) under their own weight. They are but remnants of the Pleistocene ice sheets when global temperatures were cooler and snow accumulated and compacted into ice.

The seasonal melting of mountain glaciers and snowfields is important today as dependable water sources for hundreds of millions of people worldwide. Glaciers continue to influence mountain climates and the plant and animal communities that live there. For example, meltwater from glaciers and permanent snowfields irrigate plant communities that animals like mountain goats and marmots graze. This steady supply of water extends the growing season of nutritious plants throughout summer and into fall. Mountain goats also seek glaciers and snowfields to regulate their body temperature and for relief from biting insects.

Glaciers are rapidly shrinking worldwide as our climate has warmed since the Industrial Revolution. In Montana, all but 25 of Glacier National Park's 150 mountain glaciers known in 1850 have disappeared. The remaining 25 may shrink so much by the year 2030 that they're no longer classified by scientists as glaciers. That will leave this spectacular landscape as un-Glacier National Park. Visit Glacier National Park's website to see photo evidence showing the loss of glaciers over the last century.

About the Author

Bruce Smith is a wildlife biologist who holds a PhD degree in Zoology. During his career, he studied and managed most large mammal species that roam the western United States. He's authored five nonfiction books of science, natural history, and outdoor adventure. Among them, *Stories from Afield* won the Great Northwest Book Festival Award and *Life on the Rocks: A Portrait of the American Mountain Goat* won the National Outdoor Book Award.

The *Legend Keepers* series takes young readers to the lofty realm of the mountain goat—a place still not remote enough to escape the ongoing climate crisis. *The Chosen One*, the first novel in the *Legend Keepers* series, won two silver medals in the Feathered Quill Book Awards. Bruce and his wife, Diana, live in southwest Montana where he writes to promote conservation of wild things and wild places. Visit him at *www.brucesmithwildlife.com.*

Nonfiction Books by Bruce Smith

Stories from Afield: Adventures with Wild Things in Wild Places (2016 University of Nebraska Press)

Life on the Rocks: A Portrait of the American Mountain Goat (2014 University Press of Colorado)

Where Elk Roam: Conservation and Biopolitics of Our National Elk Herd (2012 Lyons Press)

Wildlife on the Wind: A Field Biologist's Journey and an Indian Reservation's Renewal (2010 Utah State University Press)

Imperfect Pasture: A Century of Change at the National Elk Refuge in Jackson Hole, Wyoming (2004 Grand Teton Natural History Association)

Fiction Books by Bruce Smith

Legend Keepers: The Chosen One (2021 Hidden Shelf Publishing House)

Acknowledgments

Long before finishing *The Chosen One*, the first book in the *Legend Keepers* series, I knew that I couldn't leave Buddy, Roark, and Oreo behind. I wanted more from them, and I hoped that the book's readers would too. But how could one small mountain goat stem a global crisis? Buddy needed help—help of the human kind. She needed a partner equally committed to protecting her home. She needed Garson, an ordinary yet remarkable boy. By choosing to open himself up to others, Garson leveraged his curiosity and passion beyond what he could accomplish alone.

This is certainly true for writing and publishing a book, even when only one name appears on the cover. Hidden Shelf Publishing House brought the *Legend Keepers* series to life. For that I thank my stalwart editor, Bob Gaines, who believed in these stories and the good they may do in elevating awareness of the climate crisis. Rachel Wickstrom and Kristen Carrico contributed to the book's making in ways that generally go unrecognized.

Aimee Stephens, Katrina Bitz, and Paula Lee advised me on the ins-and-outs of science fair competitions. As teachers, they are vital partners in developing our children's minds.

Dan Fagre reviewed those chapters in which Garson made his studies of the glacier. So good to have a world-class glaciologist ensure that I didn't stray too far from the ice. And Anna Sala indulged me in discussions about calculating how much carbon is stored in forest stands. Perhaps Kira will forgive her for that.

My wife and advocate, Diana, reviewed each draft chapter and once again created the evocative artwork on the book's cover. Thanks, my love, for your support.

Less than one percent of Americans serve their country in the military. Families of a fraction of those experience the loss of a loved one in combat. I wanted readers to glimpse what a child of a parent who doesn't return from war may feel. For insight beyond my personal experience as a combat Marine in Vietnam, I turned to Marine Staff Sergeants Andrew Hoopii and Bryan Smith for discussions on the most unfathomable of tragedies. Yet as *Legend Keepers* continues, hope survives with passion and a plan.

Book Three Coming Soon

The Promise

Garson is determined to keep his promise to Buddy, even as Roark chides her, "Maybe there's nothing goats and ravens can do to change the future. And whatever makes you think *that boy* can?" But never underestimate a twelve-year-old with a plan. There's nothing Garson wants more than to protect Shining Mountain. Nothing except to see his dad again, and perhaps Buddy.

Made in the USA
Middletown, DE
10 November 2024

64040945R00121